CALL ME
MRS. MIRACLE

CALL ME
MRS. MIRACLE

DEBBIE MACOMBER

THORNDIKE
CHIVERS

LIBRARY OF CONGRESS CATALOGING-IN-PUBLICATION DATA

Macomber, Debbie.
  Call me Mrs. Miracle / by Debbie Macomber.
    p. cm. — (Thorndike Press large print basic)
  ISBN-13: 978-1-4104-3090-8 (hardcover)
  ISBN-10: 1-4104-3090-1 (hardcover)
  1. Women sales personnel—Fiction. 2. Christmas stories.
3. New York (N.Y.)—Fiction. 4. Large type books. I. Title.
PS3563.A2364C35 2010b
813—.54—dc22   2010031368

BRITISH LIBRARY CATALOGUING-IN-PUBLICATION DATA AVAILABLE
Published in the U.S. in 2010 in arrangement with Harlequin Books S.A.
Published in the U.K. in 2011 by arrangement with Harlequin Enterprises II B.V.
U.K. Hardcover: 978 1 408 49323 6 (Chivers Large Print)
U.K. Softcover: 978 1 408 49324 3 (Camden Large Print)

Printed in the United States of America
1 2 3 4 5 6 7 14 13 12 11 10

To
Dan and Sally Wigutow
and
Caroline Moore
in appreciation for bringing
Mrs. Miracle
to life

Christmas 2010

Dear Friends,

After the success of *Mrs. Miracle,* the Hallmark movie released last Christmas, I was asked to write a sequel. Naturally everyone wanted the story to be the same . . . only different. No pressure, right? Then I thought about one of my all-time favorite Christmas movies — *Miracle on 34th Street.* Hmm . . . can't you just imagine my Mrs. Miracle working in the toy department of a major department store in New York? That's when my mind started popping with ideas.

So here is *Call Me Mrs. Miracle* — the same, only different. I know you're going to enjoy the story, and if everything works out according to schedule (which may require a few miracles of its own), this sequel will also be a Hallmark movie slated for December.

I've dedicated the book to Dan and Sally Wigutow. Dan is the movie producer who brought Mrs. Miracle to life last December on the Hallmark channel. Sally is his wife, whom I've had the pleasure of meeting. Dan is a wise man to have chosen such a wonderful, insightful woman. Caroline Moore is Dan's co-producer and was the first one to give Dan my book. "We need to turn this into a movie," she told him. The woman is brilliant . . . but then what else can I say?

Getting this project together quickly has been a challenge and I owe a debt of appreciation to my editor, who worked long hours on this manuscript to whip it into shape in time to hand it off to Dan to get it to the screenplay writer to get it back to Dan and Hallmark . . . you've got the idea. Thank you, Paula.

A huge note of gratitude to Jody Hotchkiss, my movie agent, who moved heaven and earth to make this deal happen so fast, and to Theresa Park, my literary agent, as well. I am surrounded by a fabulous team.

Now the book is in the hands of the

most important people of all, and that's you, my readers. Sit back, enjoy and celebrate the season.

Christmas greetings.

Debbie Macomber

P.S. As always, I'd love to hear your thoughts and reactions. You can reach me at www.debbiemacomber.com or P.O. Box 1458, Port Orchard, WA 98366.

ONE

Need a new life?
God takes trade-ins.
— Mrs. Miracle

Jake Finley waited impatiently to be ushered into his father's executive office — the office that would one day be his. The thought of eventually stepping into J. R. Finley's shoes excited him. Even though he'd slowly been working his way through the ranks, he'd be the first to admit he still had a lot to learn. However, he was willing to do whatever it took to prove himself.

Finley's was the last of the family-owned department stores in New York City. His great-grandfather had begun the small mercantile on East 34th Street more than seventy years earlier. In the decades since, succeeding Finleys had opened branches in the other boroughs and then in nearby towns. Eventually the chain had spread up

11

and down the East Coast.

"Your father will see you now," Mrs. Coffey said. Dora Coffey had served as J.R.'s executive assistant for at least twenty-five years and knew as much about the company as Jake did — maybe more. He hoped that when the time came she'd stay on, although she had to be close to retirement age.

"Thank you." He walked into the large office with its panoramic view of the Manhattan skyline. He'd lived in the city all his life, but this view never failed to stir him, never failed to lift his heart. No place on earth was more enchanting than New York in December. He could see a light snow drifting down, and the city appeared even more magical through that delicate veil.

Jacob R. Finley, however, wasn't looking at the view. His gaze remained focused on the computer screen. And his frown told Jake everything he needed to know.

He cleared his throat, intending to catch J.R.'s attention, although he suspected that his father was well aware of his presence. "You asked to see me?" he said. Now that he was here, he had a fairly good idea what had initiated this summons. Jake had hoped it wouldn't happen quite so soon, but he should've guessed Mike Scott would go running to his father at the first opportunity.

Unfortunately, Jake hadn't had enough time to prove that he was right — and Mike was wrong.

"How many of those SuperRobot toys did you order?" J.R. demanded, getting straight to the point. His father had never been one to lead gently into a subject. "Intellytron," he added scornfully.

"Also known as Telly," Jake said in a mild voice.

"How many?"

"Five hundred." As if J.R. didn't know.

"What?"

Jake struggled not to flinch at his father's angry tone, which was something he rarely heard. They had a good relationship, but until now, Jake hadn't defied one of his father's experienced buyers.

"For how many stores?"

"Just here."

J.R.'s brow relaxed, but only slightly. "Do you realize those things retail for two hundred and fifty dollars apiece?"

J.R. knew the answer to that as well as Jake did. "Yes."

His father stood and walked over to the window, pacing back and forth with long, vigorous strides. Although in his early sixties, J.R. was in excellent shape. Tall and lean, like Jake himself, he had dark hair streaked with gray and his features were well-defined. No one could doubt that they were father and son. J.R. whirled around, hands linked behind him. "Did you clear the order with . . . anyone?"

Jake was as straightforward as his father. "No."

"Any particular reason you went over Scott's head?"

Jake had a very good reason. "We discussed it. He didn't agree, but I felt this was the right thing to do." Mike Scott had wanted to bring a maximum of fifty robots into the Manhattan location. Jake had tried to persuade him, but Mike wasn't interested in listening to speculation or taking what he saw as a risk — one that had the potential of leaving them with a huge overstock. He relied on cold, hard figures and years of purchasing experience. When their discussion was over, Mike still refused to go against what he considered his own better judgment. Jake continued to argue, presenting internet research and what his gut was telling him about this toy. When he'd finished, Mike Scott had countered with a list of reasons why fifty units per store would be adequate. *More* than adequate, in his opinion. While Jake couldn't disagree with the other man's logic, he had a strong hunch that the much larger order was worth the risk.

"You *felt* it was right?" his father repeated in a scathing voice. "Mike Scott told me we'd be fortunate to sell fifty in each store, yet you, with your vast experience of two months in the toy department, decided the Manhattan store needed ten times that number."

Jake didn't have anything to add.

"I don't suppose you happened to notice that there's been a downturn in the economy? Parents don't *have* two hundred and fifty bucks for a toy. Not when a lot of families are pinching pennies."

"You made me manager of the toy department." Jake wasn't stupid or reckless. "I'm convinced we'll sell those robots before Christmas." As manager, it was his responsibility — and his right — to order as he deemed fit. And if that meant overriding a buyer's decision — well, he could live with that.

"You think you can sell *all* five hundred of those robots?" Skepticism weighted each word. "In two weeks?"

"Yes." Jake had to work hard to maintain his air of confidence. Still he held firm.

His father took a moment to consider Jake's answer, walking a full circle around his desk as he did. "As of this morning, how many units have you sold?"

That was an uncomfortable question and Jake glanced down at the floor. "Three."

"Three." J.R. shook his head and stalked to the far side of the room, then back again as if debating how to address the situation. "So what you're saying is that our storeroom has four hundred and ninety-seven expensive SuperRobots clogging it up?"

"They're going to sell, Dad."

"It hasn't happened yet, though, has it?"

"No, but I believe the robot's going to be the hottest toy of the season. I've done the research — this is the toy kids are talking about."

"Maybe, but let me remind you, *kids* aren't our customers. Their parents are. Which is why no one else in the industry shares your opinion."

"I know it's a risk, Dad, but it's a calculated one. Have faith."

His father snorted harshly at the word *faith*. "My faith died along with your mother and sister," he snapped.

Involuntarily Jake's eyes sought out the photograph of his mother and sister. Both had been killed in a freak car accident on Christmas Eve twenty-one years ago. Neither Jake nor his father had celebrated

Christmas since that tragic night. Ironically, the holiday season was what kept Finley's in the black financially. Without the three-month Christmas shopping craze, the department-store chain would be out of business.

Because of the accident, Jake and his father ignored anything to do with Christmas in their personal lives. Every December twenty-fourth, soon after the store closed, the two of them got on a plane and flew to Saint John in the Virgin Islands. From the time Jake was twelve, there hadn't been a Christmas tree or presents or anything else that would remind him of the holiday. Except, of course, at the store. . . .

"Trust me in this, Dad," Jake pleaded. "Telly the SuperRobot will be the biggest seller of the season, and pretty soon Finley's will be the only store in Manhattan where people can find them."

His father reached for a pen and rolled it between his fingers as he mulled over Jake's words. "I put you in charge of the toy department because I thought it would be a valuable experience for you. One day you'll sit in this chair. The fate of the company will rest in your hands."

His father wasn't telling him anything Jake didn't already know.

"If the toy department doesn't show a profit because you went over Mike Scott's head, then you'll have a lot to answer for." He locked eyes with Jake. "Do I make myself clear?"

Jake nodded. If the toy department reported a loss as a result of his judgment, his father would question Jake's readiness to take over the company.

"Got it," Jake assured his father.

"Good. I want a report on the sale of that robot every week until Christmas."

"You'll have it," Jake promised. He turned to leave.

"I hope you're right about this toy, son," J.R. said as Jake opened the office door. "You've taken a big risk. I hope it pays off."

He wasn't the only one. Still, Jake believed. He'd counted on having proof that the robots were selling by the time his father learned what he'd done. Black Friday, the day after Thanksgiving, which was generally the biggest shopping day of the year, had been a major disappointment. He'd fantasized watching the robots fly off the shelves.

It hadn't happened.

Although they'd been prominently displayed, just one of the expensive toys had sold. He supposed his father had a point; in a faltering economy, people were evaluating their Christmas budgets, so toys, especially expensive ones, had taken a hit. Children might want the robots but it was their parents who did the buying.

Jake's head throbbed as he made his way to the toy department. In his rush to get to the store that morning, he'd skipped his usual stop at a nearby Starbucks. He needed his caffeine fix.

"Welcome to Finley's. May I be of assistance?" an older woman asked him. The store badge pinned prominently on her neat gray cardigan told him her name was Mrs. Emily Miracle. Her smile was cheerful and engaging. She must be the new sales assistant Human Resources had been promising him — but she simply wouldn't do. Good grief, what were they thinking up in HR? Sales in the toy department could be brisk, demanding hours of standing, not to mention dealing with cranky kids and short-tempered parents. He needed someone young. Energetic.

"What can I show you?" the woman asked.

Jake blinked, taken aback by her question. "I beg your pardon?"

"Are you shopping for one of your children?"

"Well, no. I —"

She didn't allow him to finish and steered

him toward the center aisle. "We have an excellent selection of toys for any age group. If you're looking for suggestions, I'd be more than happy to help."

She seemed completely oblivious to the fact that he was the department manager — and therefore her boss. "Excuse me, Mrs. . . ." He glanced at her name tag a second time. "Mrs. Miracle."

"Actually, it's Merkle."

"The badge says Miracle."

"Right," she said, looking a bit chagrined. "HR made a mistake, but I don't mind. You can call me Mrs. Miracle."

Speaking of miracles . . . If ever Jake needed one, it was now. Those robots *had* to sell. His entire future with the company could depend on this toy.

"I'd be more than happy to assist you," Mrs. Miracle said again, breaking into his thoughts.

"I'm Jake Finley."

"Pleased to meet you. Do you have a son or a daughter?" she asked.

"This is *Finley's* Department Store," he said pointedly.

Apparently this new employee had yet to make the connection, which left Jake wondering exactly where HR found their seasonal help. There had to be someone more capable than this woman.

"Finley," Mrs. Miracle repeated slowly. "Jacob Robert is your father, then?"

"Yes," he said, frowning. Only family and close friends knew his father's middle name.

Her eyes brightened, and a smile slid into place. "Ahh," she said knowingly.

"You're acquainted with my father?" That could explain why she'd been hired. Maybe she had some connection to his family he knew nothing about.

"No, no, not directly, but I *have* heard a great deal about him."

So had half the population on the East Coast. "I'm the manager here in the toy department," he told her. He clipped on his badge as he spoke, realizing he'd stuck it in his pocket. The badge said simply "Manager," without including his name, since his policy was to be as anonymous as possible, to be known by his role, not his relationship to the owner.

"The manager. Yes," she said, nodding happily. "This works out beautifully."

"What does?" Her comments struck him as odd.

"Oh, nothing," she returned with the same smile.

She certainly looked pleased with herself, although Jake couldn't imagine why. He

21

doubted she'd last a week. He'd see about getting her transferred to a more suitable department for someone her age. Oh, he'd be subtle about it. He had no desire to risk a discrimination suit.

Jake examined the robot display, hoping that while he'd been gone another one might have sold. But if that was the case, he didn't see any evidence of it.

"Have you had your morning coffee?" Mrs. Miracle asked.

"No," he muttered. His head throbbed, reminding him of his craving for caffeine.

"It seems quiet here at the moment. Why don't you take your break?" she suggested. "The other sales associate and I can handle anything that comes along."

Jake hesitated.

"Go on," she urged. "Everyone needs their morning coffee."

"You go," he said. He was, after all, the department manager, so he should be the last to leave.

"Oh, heavens, no. I just finished a cup." Looking around, she gestured toward the empty aisles. "It's slow right now but it's sure to pick up later, don't you think?"

She was right. In another half hour or so, he might not get a chance. His gaze rested on the robots and he pointed in their direction. "Do what you can to interest shoppers in those."

"Telly the SuperRobot?" she said. Not waiting for his reply, she added, "You won't have any worries there. They're going to be the hottest item this Christmas."

Jake felt a surge of excitement. "You heard that?"

"No . . ." she answered thoughtfully.

"Then you must've seen a news report." Jake had been waiting for exactly this kind of confirmation. He'd played a hunch, taken a chance, and in his heart of hearts felt it had been a good decision. But he had four hundred and ninety-seven of these robots on his hands. If his projections didn't pan out, it would take a long time — like maybe forever — to live it down.

"Coffee," Mrs. Miracle said, without explaining why she was so sure of the robot's success.

Jake checked his watch, then nodded. "I'll be back soon."

"Take whatever time you need."

Jake thanked her and hurriedly left, stopping by HR on his way out. The head of the department, Gloria Palmer, glanced up when Jake entered the office. "I've got a new woman on the floor this morning. Emily Miracle," he said.

Gloria frowned. "Miracle?" She tapped some keys on her computer and looked back at Jake. "I don't show anyone with that name working in your department."

Jake remembered that Emily Miracle had said there'd been an error on her name tag. He rubbed his hand across his forehead, momentarily closing his eyes as he tried to remember the name she'd mentioned. "It starts with an *M* — McKinsey, Merk, something like that."

Gloria's phone rang and she reached for it, holding it between her shoulder and ear as her fingers flew across the keyboard. She tried to divide her attention between Jake and the person on the line. Catching Jake's eye, she motioned toward the computer screen, shrugged and shook her head.

Jake raised his hand and mouthed, "I'll catch you later."

Gloria nodded and returned her attention to the caller. Clearly she had more pressing issues to attend to just then. Jake would seek her out later that afternoon and suggest Mrs. Miracle be switched to another department. A less demanding one.

As he rushed out the door onto Thirty-fourth and headed into the still-falling snow, he decided it would be only fair to give the older woman a chance. If she managed to sell one of the robots while he collected his morning cup of java, he'd consider keeping her. And if she managed to sell *two,* she'd be living up to her name!

Two

If God is your copilot, trade places.
                                    — Mrs. Miracle

Friday morning, and Holly Larson was right on schedule — even a few minutes ahead. This was a vast improvement over the past two months, ever since her eight-year-old nephew, Gabe, had come to live with her. It'd taken effort on both their parts to make this arrangement work. Mickey, Holly's brother, had been called up by the National Guard and sent to Afghanistan for the next fifteen months. He was a widower, and with her parents doing volunteer medical work in Haiti, the only option for Gabe was to move in with Holly, who lived in a small Brooklyn apartment. Fortunately, she'd been able to turn her minuscule home office into a bedroom for Gabe.

They were doing okay, but it hadn't been easy. Never having spent much time with children Gabe's age, the biggest adjustment had been Holly's — in her opinion, anyway.

Gabe might not agree, however. He didn't think sun-dried tomatoes with fresh mozzarella cheese was a special dinner. He turned up his nose and refused even one bite. So she was learning. Boxed macaroni and cheese suited him just fine, although she couldn't tolerate the stuff. At least it was cheap. Adding food for a growing boy to her already strained budget had been a challenge. Mickey, who was the manager of a large grocery store in his civilian life, sent what he could but he had his own financial difficulties; she knew he was still paying off his wife's medical bills and funeral expenses. And he had a mortgage to maintain on his Trenton, New Jersey, home. Poor Gabe. The little boy had lost his mother when he was an infant. Now his father was gone, too. Holly considered herself a poor replacement for either parent, let alone both, although she was giving it her best shot.

Since she had a few minutes to spare before she was due at the office, she hurried into Starbucks to reward herself with her favorite latte. It'd been two weeks since she'd had one. A hot, freshly brewed latte was an extravagance these days, so she only bought them occasionally.

Getting Gabe to school and then hurrying to the office was as difficult as collecting him from the after-school facility at the end of the day. Lindy Lee, her boss, hadn't taken kindly to Holly's rushing out the instant the clock struck five. But the child-care center at Gabe's school charged by the minute when she was late. *By the minute.*

Stepping out of the cold into the warmth of the coffee shop, Holly breathed in the pungent scent of fresh coffee. A cheery evergreen swag was draped across the display case. She dared not look because she had a weakness for cranberry scones. She missed her morning ritual of a latte and a scone almost as much as she did her independence. But giving it up was a small sacrifice if it meant she could help her brother and Gabe. Not only that, she'd come to adore her young nephew and, despite everything, knew she'd miss him when her brother returned.

The line moved quickly, and she placed her order for a skinny latte with vanilla flavoring. The man behind her ordered a large coffee. He smiled at her and Holly smiled back. She'd seen him in this Starbucks before, although they'd never spoken.

"Merry Christmas," she said.

"Same to you."

28

The girl at the cash register told Holly her total and she opened her purse to pay. That was when she remembered — she'd given the last of her cash to Gabe for lunch money. It seemed ridiculous to use a credit card for such a small amount, but she didn't have any choice. She took out her card and handed it to the barista. The young woman slid it through the machine, then leaned forward and whispered, "It's been declined."

Hot embarrassment reddened her face. She'd maxed out her card the month before but thought her payment would've been credited by now. Scrambling, she searched for coins in the bottom of her purse. It didn't take her long to realize she didn't have nearly enough change to cover the latte. "I have a debit card in here some-place," she muttered, grabbing her card case again.

"Excuse me." The good-looking man behind her pulled his wallet from his hip pocket.

"I'm . . . I'm sorry," she whispered, unable to meet his eyes. This was embarrassing, humiliating, downright mortifying.

"Allow me to pay for your latte," he said.

Holly sent him a shocked look. "You don't need to do that."

The woman standing behind him frowned

impatiently at Holly. "If I'm going to get to work on time, he does."

"Oh, sorry."

Not waiting for her to agree, the stranger stepped forward and paid for both her latte and his coffee.

"Thank you," she said in a low, strangled voice.

"I'll consider it my good deed for the day."

"I'll pay for your coffee the next time I see you."

He grinned. "You've got a deal." He moved down to the end of the counter where she went to wait for her latte. "I'm Jake Finley."

"Holly Larson." She extended her hand.

"Holly," he repeated.

"People assume I was born around Christmas but I wasn't. Actually, I was born in June and named after my mother's favorite aunt," she said. She didn't know why she'd blurted out such ridiculous information. Perhaps because she still felt embarrassed and was trying to disguise her chagrin with conversation. "I do love Christmas, though, don't you?"

"Not particularly." Frowning, he glanced at his watch. "I've got to get back to work."

"Oh, sure. Thank you again." He'd been thoughtful and generous.

30

"See you soon," Jake said as he turned toward the door.

"I owe you," she said. "I won't forget."

He smiled at her. "I hope I'll run into you again."

"That would be great." She meant it, and next time she'd make sure she had enough cash to treat him. She felt a glow of pleasure as Jake left Starbucks.

Holly stopped to calculate — it'd been more than three months since her last date. That was pitiful! Three months. Nuns had a more active social life than she did.

Her last relationship had been with Bill Carter. For a while it had seemed promising. As a divorced father, Bill was protective and caring toward his young son. Holly had only met Billy once. Unfortunately, the trip to the Central Park Zoo hadn't gone well. Billy had been whiny and overtired, and Bill had seemed to want *her* to deal with the boy. She'd tried but Billy didn't know her and she didn't know him, and the entire outing had been strained and uncomfortable. Holly had tried — unsuccessfully — to make the trip as much fun as possible. Shortly thereafter, Bill called to tell her their relationship wasn't "working" for him. He'd made a point of letting her know he was interested in finding someone more "suitable" for his son because he didn't feel she'd make a good mother. His words had stung.

Holly hadn't argued. Really, how could she? Her one experience with Billy had been a disaster. Then, just a month after Bill's heartless comment, Gabe had entered her life. These days she was more inclined to agree with Bill's assessment of her parenting skills. She didn't seem to have what it took to raise a child, which deeply concerned her.

Things were getting easier with Gabe, but progress had been slow, and it didn't help that her nephew seemed to sense her unease. She had a lot to learn about being an effective and nurturing parent.

Dating Bill had been enjoyable enough, but there'd never been much chemistry between them, so not seeing him wasn't a huge loss. She categorized it as more of a disappointment. A letdown. His parting words, however, had left her with doubts and regrets.

Carrying her latte, Holly walked the three blocks to the office. She actually arrived a minute early. Working as an assistant to a fashion designer sounded glamorous but it wasn't. She didn't get to take home designer purses for a fraction of their retail price — except for the knockoff versions she could buy on the street — or acquire fashion-model hand-me-downs.

She was paid a pittance and had become the go-to person for practically everyone on staff, and that added up to at least forty people. Her boss, Lindy Lee, was often unreasonable. Unfortunately, most of the time it was Holly's job to make sure that whatever Lindy wanted actually happened. Lindy wasn't much older than Holly, but she was well connected in the fashion world and had quickly risen to the top. Because her work as a designer of upscale women's sportswear was in high demand, Lindy Lee frequently worked under impossible deadlines. One thing was certain; she had no tolerance for the fact that Holly now had to stick to her official nine-to-five schedule, which meant her job as Lindy Lee's assistant might be in jeopardy. She'd explained the situation with Gabe, but her boss didn't care about Holly's problems at home.

Rushing to her desk, Holly set the latte down, shrugged off her coat and readied herself for the day. She was responsible for decorating the office for Christmas, and so far, there just hadn't been time. On Saturday she'd bring Gabe into the office and the two of them would get it done. That meant her own apartment would have to wait, but . . . oh, well.

Despite her boss's complaints about one thing or another, Holly's smile stayed in place all morning. A kind deed by a virtual stranger buffered her from four hours of commands, criticism and complaints.

Jack . . . no, Jake. He'd said his name was Jake, and he was cute, too. Maybe *handsome* was a more accurate description. Classically handsome, like those 1940s movie stars in the old films she loved. Tall, nicely trimmed dark hair, broad shoulders, expressive eyes and . . . probably married. She'd been too shocked by his generosity to see whether he had a wedding band. Yeah, he was probably taken. Par for the course, she thought a little glumly. Holly was thirty, but being single at that age wasn't uncommon among her friends. Her parents seemed more worried about it than she was.

Most of her girlfriends didn't even *think* about settling down until after they turned thirty. Holly knew she wanted a husband and eventually a family. What she hadn't expected was becoming a sole parent to Gabe. This time with her nephew was like a dress rehearsal for being a mother, her friends told her. Unfortunately, there weren't any lines to memorize and the script changed almost every day.

At lunch she heated her Cup-a-Soup in the microwave and logged on to the internet to check for messages from Mickey. Her brother kept in touch with Gabe every day and sent her a quick note whenever he could. Sure enough, there was an email waiting for her.

From: "Lieutenant Mickey Larson"
  <larsonmichael@goarmy.com>
To: "Holly Larson"
  <hollylarson@msm.com>
Sent: December 10
Subject: Gabe's email

Hi, sis,
Gabe's last note to me was hilarious. What's this about you making him put down the toilet seat? He thinks girls should do it themselves. This is what happens when men live together. The seat's perpetually up.
Has he told you what he wants for Christmas yet? He generally mentions a toy before now, but he's been suspiciously quiet about it this year. Let me know when he drops his hints.
I wish I could be with you both, but that's out of the question. Next year for sure.

I know it's been rough on you having to fit Gabe into your apartment and your life, but I have no idea what I would've done without you.

By the way, I heard from Mom and Dad. The dental clinic Dad set up is going well. Who'd have guessed our parents would be doing volunteer work after retirement? They send their love . . . but now that I think about it, you got the same email as me, didn't you? They both sound happy but really busy. Mom was concerned about you taking Gabe, but she seems reassured now.

Well, I better get some shut-eye. Not to worry — I reminded Gabe that when he's staying at a house with a woman living in it, the correct thing to do is put down the toilet seat.

Check in with you later.

Thank you again for everything.

Love,
Mickey

Holly read the message twice, then sent him a note. She'd always been close to her brother and admired him for picking up the pieces of his life after Sally died of a rare blood disease. Gabe hadn't even been a year old. Holly had a lot more respect for the demands of parenthood — and especially single parenthood — now that Gabe lived with her.

At five o'clock, she was out the door. Lindy Lee threw her an evil look, which Holly pretended not to see. She caught the subway and had to stand, holding tight to one of the poles, for the whole rush-hour ride into Brooklyn.

As she was lurched and jolted on the train, her mind wandered back to Mickey's email. Gabe hadn't said anything about Christmas to her, either. And yet he had to know that the holidays were almost upon them; all the decorations in the neighborhood and the ads on TV made it hard to miss. For the first time in his life, Gabe wouldn't be spending Christmas with his father and grandparents. This year, there'd be just the two of them. Maybe he'd rather not celebrate until his father came home, she thought. That didn't seem right, though. Holly was determined to make this the best Christmas possible.

Not once had Gabe told her what he wanted. She wondered whether she should ask him, maybe encourage him to write Santa a letter — did he still believe in Santa? — or try to guess what he might like. Her other question was what she could buy on a limited income. A toy? She knew next to nothing about toys, especially the kind that would intrigue an eight-year-old boy. She felt besieged by even more insecurities.

She stepped off the subway, climbed the stairs to the street and hurried to Gabe's school, which housed the after-hours activity program set up for working parents. At least it wasn't snowing anymore. Which was a good thing, since she'd forgotten to make Gabe wear his boots that morning.

What happened the first day she'd gone to collect Gabe still made her cringe. She'd been thirty-two minutes late. The financial penalty was steep and cut into her carefully planned budget, but that didn't bother her nearly as much as the look on Gabe's face.

He must have assumed she'd abandoned him. His haunted expression brought her to the edge of tears every time she thought about it. That was the same night she'd prepared her favorite dinner for him — another disaster. Now she knew better and kept an unending supply of hot dogs — God help them both — plus boxes of macaroni and cheese. He'd deign to eat carrot sticks and bananas, but those were his only concessions, no matter how much she talked about balanced nutrition. He found it hilarious to claim that the relish he slathered on his hot dogs was a "vegetable."

She waited by the row of hooks, each marked with a child's name. Gabe ran over the instant he saw her, his face bright with excitement. "I made a new friend!"

"That's great." Thankfully Gabe appeared to have adjusted well to his new school and teacher.

"Billy!" he called. "Come and meet my aunt Holly."

Holly's smile froze. This wasn't just any Billy. It was Bill Carter, Junior, son of the man who'd broken up with her three months earlier.

"Hello, Billy," she said, wondering if he'd recognize her.

The boy gazed up at her quizzically. Apparently he didn't. Or maybe he did remember her but wasn't sure when they'd met. Either way, Holly was relieved.

"Can I go over to Billy's house?" Gabe asked. The two boys linked arms like long-lost brothers.

"Ah, when?" she hedged. Seeing Bill again would be difficult. Holly wasn't eager to talk to the man who'd dumped her — especially considering why. It would be uncomfortable for both of them.

"I want him to come tonight," Billy said. "My dad's making sloppy joes. And we've got marshmallow ice cream for dessert."

"Well . . ." Her meals could hardly compete with that — not if you were an eight-year-old boy. Personally, Holly couldn't think of a less appetizing combination.

Before she could come up with a response, Gabe tugged at her sleeve. "Billy doesn't have a mom, either," he told her.

"I have a mom," Billy countered, "only she doesn't live with us anymore."

"My mother's in heaven with the angels," Gabe said. "I live with my dad, too, 'cept he's in Afghanistan now."

"So that's why you're staying with your aunt Holly." Billy nodded.

"Yeah." Gabe reached for his jacket and backpack.

"I'm sorry, Billy," she finally managed to say, "but Gabe and I already have plans for tonight."

Gabe whirled around. "We do?"

"We're going shopping," she said, thinking on her feet.

Gabe scowled and crossed his arms. "I hate shopping."

"You won't this time," she promised and helped him put on his winter jacket, along with his hat and mitts.

"Yes, I will," Gabe insisted, his head lowered.

"You and Billy can have a playdate later," she said, forcing herself to speak cheerfully.

"When?" Billy asked, unwilling to let the matter drop.

"How about next week?" She'd call or email Bill so it wouldn't come as a big shock when she showed up on his doorstep.

"Okay," Billy agreed.

"That suit you?" Holly asked Gabe. She wanted to leave *now,* just in case Bill was picking up his son today. She recalled that their housekeeper usually did this — but why take chances? Bill was the very last person she wanted to see.

Gabe shrugged, unhappy with the compromise. He let her take his hand as they left the school, but as soon as they were outdoors, he promptly snatched it away.

"Where are we going shopping?" he asked, still pouting as they headed in the opposite direction of her apartment building. The streetlights glowed and she saw Christmas decorations in apartment windows — wreaths, small potted trees and strings of colored lights. So far Holly hadn't done anything. Perhaps this weekend she'd find time to put up their tree — after she'd finished decorating the office, of course.

"I thought we'd go see Santa this evening," Holly announced.

41

"Santa?" He raised his head and eyed her speculatively.

"Would you like that?"

Gabe seemed to need a moment to consider the question. "I guess."

Holly assumed he was past the age of believing in Santa but wasn't quite ready to admit it, for fear of losing out on extra gifts. Still, she didn't feel she could ask him. "I want you to hold my hand while we're on the subway, okay?"

"Okay," he said in a grumpy voice.

They'd go to Finley's, she decided. She knew for sure that the store had a Santa. Besides, she wanted to look at the windows with their festive scenes and moving parts. Even in his current mood, Gabe would enjoy them, Holly thought. And so would she.

THREE

Exercise daily — walk with the Lord.
                                    — Mrs. Miracle

It was the second Friday in December and the streets were crowded with shoppers and tourists. As they left the subway, Holly kept a close watch on Gabe, terrified of becoming separated. She heaved a sigh of relief when they reached Finley's Department Store. The big display windows in the front of the fourteen-story structure were cleverly decorated. One showed a Santa's workshop scene, including animated elves wielding hammers and saws. Another was a mirrored pond that had teddy bears skating around and around. Still another, the window closest to the doors, featured a huge Christmas tree, circled by a toy train running on its own miniature track. The boxcars were filled with gaily wrapped gifts.

With the crowds pressing against them,

Gabe and Holly moved from window to window, stopping at the final one. "Isn't that a great train set?" she asked.

Gabe nodded.

"Would you like one of those for Christmas?" she murmured. "You could ask Santa."

Gabe glanced up at her. "There's something else I want more."

"Okay, you can tell Santa that," she said.

They headed into the store, and had difficulty getting through the revolving doors, crushed in with other shoppers. "Can we go home and have dinner when we're done seeing Santa?" Gabe asked.

"Of course. What would you like?"

If he said hot dogs or macaroni and cheese Holly promised herself she wouldn't scream.

"Mashed potatoes with gravy and meat loaf with lots of ketchup."

That would take a certain amount of effort but was definitely something she could do. "You got it."

Gabe cast her one of his rare smiles, and Holly placed her hand on his shoulder. This was progress.

The ground floor of Finley's was crammed. The men's department was to the right and the cosmetics and perfume counters directly ahead. Holly inched her way forward, Gabe close by her side.

"We need to get to the escalator," she told him, steering the boy in that direction. She hoped that once they got up to the third floor, the crowds would have thinned out, at least a little.

"Okay." He voluntarily slipped his hand in hers.

More progress. Visiting Santa had clearly been a stroke of genius on her part.

Her guess about the crowds was accurate. When they reached the third floor Holly felt she could breathe again. If it wasn't for Gabe, she wouldn't come within ten miles of Thirty-fourth on a Friday night in December.

"Santa's over there," Gabe said, pointing.

The kid obviously had Santa Claus radar. Several spry elves in green tights and pointy hats surrounded the jolly old man in the red suit. This guy was good, too. His full white beard was real. He must've just gotten off break because he wore a huge smile.

The visit to Santa was free but for an extra twenty dollars, she could buy a picture. They'd stopped at an ATM on their way to the subway and she'd gotten cash. Although she couldn't help feeling a twinge at spending the money, a photo of Gabe with Santa would be the perfect Christmas gift for Mickey.

The line moved quickly. Gabe seemed excited and happy, chattering away about this and that, and his mood infected Holly. She hadn't felt much like Christmas until now. Classic carols rang through the store and soon Holly was humming along.

When it was Gabe's turn, he hopped onto Santa's knee as if the two of them were old friends.

"Hello there, young man," Santa said, adding a "Ho, ho, ho."

"Hello." Gabe looked him square in the eyes.

"And what would you like Santa to bring you?" the jolly old fellow inquired.

Her nephew didn't hesitate. "All I want for Christmas is Telly the SuperRobot."

What in heaven's name was that? A robot? Even without checking, Holly knew this wasn't going to be a cheap toy. A train set — a small one — she could manage, but an electronic toy was probably out of her price range.

"Very well, young man, Santa will see what he can do. Anything else you're interested in?"

"A train set," Gabe said, his eyes serious. "But I *really* want Intellytron."

"Intellytron," Holly muttered to herself.

Santa gestured at the camera. "Now smile big for me, and your mom can collect the photograph in five minutes."

"Okay." Gabe gave Santa a huge smile, then slid off his knee so the next child in line could have a turn. It took Holly a moment to realize that Gabe hadn't corrected Santa about who she was.

Holly went around to the counter behind Santa's chair to wait for the photograph, accompanied by Gabe.

"I don't know where Santa will find one of those robots," she said, trying to get as much information as she could.

"All the stores have them," Gabe assured her. "Billy wants an Intellytron, too."

So she could blame Billy for this sudden desire. But since this was the only toy Gabe wanted, she'd do her best to make sure that Intellytron the SuperRobot would be wrapped and under the tree Christmas morning.

"Maybe I should see what this robot friend of yours looks like," she suggested. A huge sign pointing to the toy department was strategically placed near Santa's residence. This, Holly felt certain, was no coincidence.

"Toys are this way," Gabe said, leading

47

her by the hand.

Holly dutifully followed. "What if they don't have the robot?" she asked.

"They will," he said with sublime confidence.

"But what if they don't?"

Gabe frowned and then tilted his chin at a thoughtful angle. "Can Santa bring my dad home?"

Holly's heart sank. "Not this year, sweetheart."

"Then all I really want is my robot."

She'd been afraid of that.

They entered the toy department and were met by a grandmotherly woman with a name badge that identified her as Mrs. Emily Miracle.

"Why, hello there," the woman greeted Gabe with a smile.

Gabe immediately smiled back at her. "Hello."

"I see you've been to visit Santa." She nodded at the photo Holly was holding.

"Yup," Gabe said happily. "He was nice."

"Did you tell Santa what you want for Christmas?"

"Intellytron the SuperRobot," he replied.

"Telly is a wonderful toy. Let me show you one."

"Please," Holly said, hoping against hope

that the robot was reasonably priced. If fate was truly with her, it would also be on sale.

Mrs. Miracle took them to a display on the other side of the department, directly across from the elevator. The robots would be the first toys seen by those stepping off. She wondered why they weren't by the escalator, but then it dawned on her. Mothers with young children usually came up via elevator. The manager of this department was no dummy.

"Look!" Gabe said, his eyes huge. "It's Telly! He's here. I told you he would be. Isn't he the best *ever?*"

"Would you like to see how he works?" the grandmotherly saleswoman asked.

"Yes, please."

Holly was impressed by Gabe's politeness, which she'd never seen to quite this degree. Well, it was December, and this was the one toy he wanted more than any other. The saleswoman took down the display model and started to demonstrate it when a male voice caught Holly's attention.

"Hello again."

She turned to face Jake, the man she'd met in Starbucks that morning. For a moment she couldn't speak. Eventually she croaked out a subdued hello.

He looked curiously at Gabe. "Your son?"

"My nephew," she said, recovering her voice. "Gabe's living with me for the next year while his father's in Afghanistan."

"Nephew," he repeated, and his eyes sparked with renewed interest.

"I brought Gabe here to visit Santa and he said that what he wants for Christmas is Intellytron the SuperRobot."

"An excellent choice. Would you like me to wrap one for you now?"

"Ah . . ." Holly paused. "I need to know how much they are first." Just looking at the toy told her she wasn't getting off cheap.

"Two hundred and fifty dollars."

Holly's hand flew to her heart. "*How* much?"

"Two hundred and fifty dollars."

"Oh." She swallowed. "Will there be a sale on these later? A big sale?"

Jake shook his head. "I doubt it."

"Oh," she said again.

Jake seemed disappointed, too.

Holly bit her lip. This was the only gift Gabe had requested. He'd indicated mild interest in a train set, but that was more at her instigation. Watching his eyes light up as the robot maneuvered itself down the aisle filled her with a sense of delight. He loved this toy and it would mean so much to him. "I get my Christmas bonus at the end of next week. Will you still have the robot then?" Never mind that Lindy Lee might be less than generous this year. . . .

"We should have plenty," Jake told her.

"Thank goodness," Holly said gratefully.

"We've sold a number today, but I brought in a large supply so you shouldn't have anything to worry about."

"Wonderful." She could hardly wait for Gabe to unwrap this special gift Christmas morning. Tonight, the spirit of Christmas had finally begun to take root in her own heart. Seeing the joy of the season in Gabe's eyes helped her accept that this year would be different but could still be good. Although she and Gabe were separated from their family, she intended to make it a Christmas the two of them would always remember.

"I want to thank you again for buying my latte this morning," she said to Jake. She was about to suggest she pay him back, because she had the cash now, but hesitated, hoping for the opportunity to return the favor and spend more time with him.

"Like I said, it was my good deed for the day."

"Do you often purchase a complete stranger a cup of coffee?"

"You're the first."

She laughed. "Then I'm doubly honored."

"Aunt Holly, did you see? Did you see Telly move?" Gabe asked, dashing to her side. "He can talk, too!"

She'd been so involved in chatting with Jake that she'd missed most of the demonstration. Other children had come over to the aisle, drawn by the robot's activities; in fact, a small crowd had formed to watch. Several boys Gabe's age were tugging at their parents' arms.

"We'll have to see what Santa brings," Holly told him.

"He'll bring me Telly, won't he?"

Holly shrugged, pretending nonchalance. "We'll have to wait and see."

"How many days until Christmas?" Gabe asked eagerly.

"Today's the tenth, so . . . fifteen days."

"That long?" He dragged out the words as if he could barely hang on all those weeks.

"The time will fly by, Gabe. I promise."

"Excuse me," Jake said as he turned to answer a customer's question. Her query was about the price of the robot, and the woman had nearly the same reaction as Holly. Two hundred and fifty dollars! A lot of money for a toy. Still, in Gabe's case it would be worth it.

Mrs. Miracle brought out the display

robot to demonstrate again, and Gabe and a second youngster watched with rapt attention. The older woman was a marvel, a natural with children.

"So, you're the manager here," Holly said once Jake was free.

He nodded. "How'd you guess?" he asked with a grin.

"Your badge, among other things." She smiled back at him. "I was just thinking how smart you were to place Santa next to the toy section."

"That wasn't my idea," Jake said. "Santa's been in that location for years."

"What about the Intellytron display across from the elevator?"

"Now, that *was* my idea."

"I thought as much."

Jake seemed pleased that she'd noticed. "I'm hoping it really takes off."

"Well, if Gabe's interest is any indication, I'm sure it will."

He seemed to appreciate her vote of confidence.

"Look!" Gabe said, grabbing Holly's hand. He pointed to a couple who were removing a boxed unit of Intellytron from the display. "My robot will still be here by Christmas, won't he?"

"Absolutely," she assured him.

Jake winked at her as Mrs. Miracle led the young couple toward the cash register.

"Hiring Mrs. Miracle was a smart move, too," she said.

"Oh, I can't really take credit for that," Jake responded.

"Well, you're lucky, then. She's exactly right for the toy department. It's like having someone's grandmother here. She's helping parents fulfill all their children's Christmas wishes."

Jack glanced at the older woman, then slowly nodded. "I guess so," he said, sounding a bit uncertain.

"Haven't you seen the way kids immediately take to her?" Holly asked.

"Not only can't I take credit for her being here, it's actually a mistake."

"A mistake," Holly echoed. "You're joking! She's *perfect*. It wouldn't surprise me if you sold out the whole toy department with her working here."

"Really?" He said this as if Holly had given him something to think about.

"I love her name, too. Mrs. Miracle — it has such a nice Christmas sound."

"That's a mistake, as well. Her name's not really Miracle. HR spelled it wrong on her badge, and I asked that it be corrected."

"Oh, let her keep the badge," Holly urged.

"Mrs. Miracle. It couldn't be more appropriate."

Jake nodded again. "Perhaps you're right."

Mrs. Miracle finished the sale and joined them. "Very nice meeting you, Gabe and Holly," she said warmly.

Holly didn't remember giving the older woman her name. Gabe must have mentioned it.

"You, too, Emily," she said.

"Oh, please," she said with a charming smile. "Just call me Mrs. Miracle."

"Okay," Gabe piped up. "We will."

FOUR

Lead me not into temptation.
I can find the way myself.
                                    — J. R. Finley

"I thought we'd bake cookies today," Holly said on Saturday morning as Gabe sat at the kitchen counter eating his breakfast cereal. When he didn't think she was looking, he picked up the bowl and slurped what was left of his milk.

"Cookies?" Gabe said, frowning. "Can't we just buy them?"

"We could," Holly answered, "but I figured it would be fun to bake them ourselves."

Gabe didn't seem convinced. "Dad and I always got ours at the store. We never had to *work* to get them."

"But it's fun," Holly insisted, unwilling to give up quite so easily. "You can roll out the dough. I even have special cookie cutters.

56

After the cookies are baked and they've cooled down, we can frost and decorate them." She'd hoped this Christmas tradition would appeal to Gabe.

He slid down from his chair and carried his bowl to the dishwasher. "Can I go on the computer?"

"Sure." Holly made an effort to hide her disappointment. She'd really hoped the two of them would bond while they were baking Christmas cookies. Later, she intended to go into the office and put up decorations — with Gabe's help. She wanted that to be fun for him, too.

Gabe moved to the alcove between the kitchen and small living room with its sofa and television. Holly was astonished at how adept the eight-year-old was on the computer. While he logged on, she brought out the eggs and flour and the rest of the ingredients for sugar cookies and set them on the kitchen counter.

Gabe obviously didn't realize she could see the computer screen from her position. She was pleased that he was writing his father a note.

From: "Gabe Larson"
    <gabelarson@msm.com>
To: "Lieutenant Mickey Larson"

<larsonmichael@goarmy.com>
Sent: December 11
Subject: Cookies

Hi, Dad,
Guess what? Aunt Holly wants me to bake cookies. Doesn't she know I'm a BOY? Boys don't bake cookies. It's bad enough that I have to put the toilet seat down for her. I hope you get home soon because I'm afraid she's going to turn me into a girl!

Gabe

Holly tried to conceal her smile. "Would you like to go into the city this afternoon?" she asked as she added the butter she'd cubed to the sugar in the mixing bowl.

Gabe turned around to look at her. "You aren't going to make me go shopping, are you?"

"No. I'll take you to my office. Wouldn't you like that?"

"Yes," he said halfheartedly.

"I have to put up a few decorations. You can help me."

"Okay." Again he showed a decided lack of enthusiasm.

"The Rockefeller Center Christmas tree is up," she told him next.

Now, that caught his interest. "Can we go ice-skating?"

"Ah . . ." Holly had never gone skating. "Maybe another time, okay?"

Gabe shrugged. "Okay. I bet Billy and his dad will take me."

The kid had no idea how much that comment irritated her. However, Holly knew she had to be an adult about it. She hadn't phoned Bill to discuss the fact that his son and her nephew were friends. She would, though, in order to arrange a playdate for the two boys.

"I thought we'd leave after lunch," she said, resuming their original conversation.

"Okay." Gabe returned to the computer and was soon involved in a game featuring beasts in some alien kingdom. Whatever it was held his attention for the next ten minutes.

Using the electric mixer, Holly blended the sugar, butter and eggs and was about to add the dry ingredients when Gabe climbed up on the stool beside her.

"I've never seen anyone make cookies before," he said.

"You can watch if you want." She made an effort to sound matter-of-fact, not revealing how pleased she was at his interest.

"When we go into the city, would it be all

59

right if we went to Finley's?" he asked.

Holly looked up. "I suppose so. Any particular reason?"

He stared at her as if it should be obvious. "I want to see Telly. He can do all kinds of tricks and stuff, and maybe Mrs. Miracle will be there."

"Oh."

"Mrs. Miracle said I could stop by anytime I want and she'd let me work the controls. She said they don't normally let kids play with the toys but she'd make an exception." He drew in a deep breath. "What's an 'exception'?"

"It means she'll allow you to do it even though other people can't."

"That's what I thought." He leaned forward and braced his elbows on the counter, nodding solemnly at this evidence of his elevated status — at least in Mrs. Miracle's view.

As soon as the dough was mixed, Holly covered it with plastic wrap and put it inside the refrigerator to chill. When she'd finished, she cleaned off the kitchen counter. "You want to lick the beaters?" she asked.

Gabe straightened and looked skeptically at the mixer. "You can do that?"

"Sure. That's one of the best parts of baking cookies."

"Okay."

She handed him one beater and took the second herself.

Gabe's eyes widened after his first lick. "Hey, this tastes *good*."

"Told you," she said with a smug smile.

"Why can't we just eat the dough? Why ruin cookies by baking 'em?"

"Well, they're not cookies unless you bake them."

"Oh."

Her response seemed to satisfy him.

"I'm going to roll the dough out in a few minutes. Would you help me decide which cookie cutters to use?"

"I guess." Gabe didn't display a lot of enthusiasm at the request.

Holly stood on tiptoe to take down the plastic bag she kept on the upper kitchen shelf. "Your grandma Larson gave these to me last year. When your dad and I were your age, we used to make sugar cookies."

Gabe sat up straighter. "You mean my dad baked cookies?"

"Every Christmas. After we decorated them, we chose special people to give them to."

Gabe was always interested in learning facts about Mickey. Every night he asked Holly to tell him a story about his father as

61

a boy. She'd run out of stories, but it didn't matter; Gabe liked hearing them again and again.

"You gave the cookies to special people? Like who?"

"Well . . ." Holly had to think about that. "Once I brought a plate of cookies to my Sunday school teacher and one year —" she paused and smiled "— I was twelve and had a crush on a boy in my class, so I brought the cookies to school for him."

"Who'd my dad give the cookies to?"

"I don't remember. You'll have to ask him."

"I will." Gabe propped his chin on one hand. "Can I take a plate of cookies to Mrs. Miracle?"

Holly was about to tell him that would be a wonderful idea, then hesitated. "The problem is, if I baked the cookies and decorated them, they'd be from me and not from you."

Gabe frowned. "I could help with cutting them out and stuff. You won't tell anyone, will you?"

"Not if you don't want me to."

"I don't want any of my friends to think I'm a sissy."

She crossed her heart. "I promise not to say a word."

"Okay, then, I'll do it." Gabe dug into the bag of cookie cutters and made his selections, removing the Christmas tree, the star and several others. Then, as if a thought had suddenly struck him, he pointed at her apron. "I don't have to put on one of those, do I?"

"You don't like my apron?"

"They're okay for girls, but not boys."

"You don't have to wear one if you'd rather not."

He shook his head adamantly.

"But you might get flour on your clothes, and your friends would guess you were baking." This was a clever argument, if she did say so herself.

Gabe nibbled on his lower lip, apparently undecided. "Then I'll change clothes. I'm not wearing any girlie apron."

"That's fine," Holly said, grinning.

The rest of the morning was spent baking and decorating cookies. Once he got started, Gabe appeared to enjoy himself. He frosted the Christmas tree with green icing and sprinkled red sugar over it.

Then, with a sideways glance at Holly, he promptly ate the cookie. She let him assume she hadn't noticed.

"Who are you giving your cookies to?" Gabe asked.

Actually, Holly hadn't thought about it. "I'm not sure." A heartbeat later, the decision was made. "Jake."

"The man in the toy department at Finley's?"

Holly nodded. "He did something kind for me on Friday. He bought my coffee."

Gabe cocked his head. "Is he your boyfriend?"

"Oh, no. But he's very nice and I want to repay him." She got two plastic plates and, together, they arranged the cookies. Holly bundled each plate in green-tinted cellophane wrap and added silver bows for a festive look.

"You ready to head into town?" she asked.

Gabe raced into his bedroom for his coat, hat and mittens. "I'm ready."

"Me, too." The truth was, Holly felt excited about seeing Jake again. Of course, there was always the possibility that he wouldn't be working today — but she had to admit she hoped he was. Her reaction surprised her; since Bill had broken off their relationship she'd been reluctant to even consider dating someone new.

Meeting Jake had been an unexpected bonus. He'd been so — She stopped abruptly. Here she was, doing it again. Jake had paid for her coffee. He was obviously a generous man . . . or he might've been in a rush to get back to the store. Either way, he'd been kind to her. But that didn't mean he was *attracted* to her. In reality it meant nada. Zilch. Zip. Gazing down at the plate of cookies, Holly felt she might be pushing this too far.

"Aunt Holly?"

She looked at her nephew, who was staring quizzically at her. "Is something wrong?" he asked.

"Oh, sorry . . . No, nothing's wrong. I was just thinking maybe I should give these cookies to someone else."

"How come?"

"I . . . I don't know."

"Give them to Jake," Gabe said without a second's doubt. "Didn't you say he bought your coffee?"

"He did." Gabe was right. The cookies were simply a way of thanking him. That was all. She was returning a kindness. With her quandary settled, they walked over to the subway station.

When they arrived at Finley's, the streets and the store were even more crowded than they'd been the night before. Again Holly kept a close eye on her nephew. She'd made a contingency plan — if they did happen to get separated, they were to meet in the toy department by the robots.

They rode up on the escalator, after braving the cosmetics aisles, with staff handing out perfume samples. Gabe held his nose, but Holly was delighted to accept several tiny vials of perfume. When they finally reached the toy department, it was far busier than it had been the previous evening. Both Gabe and Holly studied the display of robots. There did seem to be fewer of the large boxes, but Jake had assured her there'd be plenty left by the time she received her Christmas bonus. She sincerely hoped that was true.

The moment Gabe saw Mrs. Miracle, he rushed to her side. "We made you sugar cookies," he said, giving her the plate.

"Oh, my, these are lovely." The grandmotherly woman smiled. "They look good enough to eat."

"You *are* supposed to eat them," Gabe said with a giggle.

"And I will." She bent down and hugged the boy. "Thank you so much."

Gabe whispered, "Don't tell anyone, but I helped Aunt Holly make them."

Holly was standing close enough to hear him and exchanged a smile with Mrs. Miracle.

"You should be proud of that," Mrs.

66

Miracle said as she led him toward the Intellytron display, holding the plate of cookies aloft. "Lots of men cook. You should have your aunt Holly turn on the Food Network so you see for yourself."

"Men bake cookies?"

"Oh, my, yes," she told him. "Now that you're here, why don't we go and show these other children how to work this special robot. You can be my assistant."

"Can I?" Wide-eyed, Gabe looked at Holly for permission.

She nodded, and Mrs. Miracle and Gabe went to the other side of the toy department. Holly noticed that Jake was busy with customers, so she wandered down a randomly chosen aisle, examining the Barbie dolls and all their accoutrements. She felt a bit foolish carrying a plate of decorated cookies.

As soon as he was free, Jake made a beeline toward her. "Hi," he said. "I didn't expect to see you again so soon."

"Hi." Looking away, she tried to explain the reason for her visit. "Gabe wanted to check out his robot again. After that, we're going to my office and then Rockefeller Center to see the Christmas tree . . . but we decided to come here first." The words tumbled out so quickly she wondered if he'd understood a thing she'd said.

He glanced at the cookies.

"These are for you," she said, shoving the plate in his direction. "Sugar cookies. In appreciation for my latte."

"Homemade sugar cookies," he murmured as if he'd never seen anything like them before.

He continued to stare at the plate for an awkward moment. Holly was afraid she'd committed a social faux pas.

"My mother used to bake sugar cookies every Christmas," Jake finally said. His eyes narrowed, and the memory seemed to bring him pain.

Holly had the absurd notion that she should apologize.

"I remember the star and the bell." He spoke in a low voice, as though transported through the years. "Oh, and look, that one's a reindeer, and of course the Christmas tree with the little cinnamon candies as ornaments."

"Gabe actually decorated that one," she said.

He looked up and his smile banished all doubt. "Thank you, Holly."

"You're welcome, Jake."

"Excuse me." A woman spoke from behind Holly. "Is there someone here who could show me the electronic games?"

Jake seemed reluctant to leave her, and Holly was loath to see him go. "I'll be happy to help you," he said. He set the cookies behind the counter and escorted the woman to another section of the department.

Holly moved to the area where Gabe and Mrs. Miracle were demonstrating Intellytron. A small crowd had gathered, and Gabe's face shone with happiness as he put the robot through its paces. In all the weeks her nephew had lived with her, she'd never seen him so excited, so fully engaged. She knew Gabe wanted this toy for Christmas; what Holly hadn't understood until this very second was just how much it meant to him.

Regardless of the cost, Holly intended to get her nephew that robot.

Holiday Sugar Cookies
(from *Debbie Macomber's Cedar Cove Cookbook*)

This foolproof sugar cookie recipe makes a sturdy, sweet treat that's a perfect gift or a great addition to a holiday cookie platter.

2 cups (4 sticks) unsalted butter, at room temperature

2 cups brown sugar

2 large eggs

2 teaspoons vanilla extract or grated lemon peel

6 cups all-purpose flour, plus extra for rolling

2 teaspoons baking powder

1 teaspoon salt

1. In a large bowl with electric mixer on medium speed, cream butter and sugar until light and fluffy. Add eggs and vanilla;

beat until combined.

2. In a separate bowl, combine flour, baking powder and salt. Reduce mixer speed to low; beat in flour mixture just until combined. Shape dough into two disks; wrap and refrigerate at least 2 hours or up to overnight.

3. Preheat oven to 350°F. Line baking sheets with parchment paper. Remove 1 dough disk from the refrigerator. Cut disk in half; cover remaining half. On a lightly floured surface with floured rolling pin, roll dough 1/4-inch thick. Using cookie cutters, cut dough into as many cookies as possible; reserve trimmings for rerolling.

4. Place cookies on prepared sheets about 1 inch apart. Bake 10 to 12 minutes (depending on the size of cookies) until pale gold. Transfer to wire rack to cool. Repeat with remaining dough and rerolled scraps.

TIP: Decorate baked cookies with prepared frosting or sprinkle unbaked cookies with colored sugars before putting them in the oven.

Makes about 48 cookies.

FIVE

People are like tea bags — you have to drop them in hot water before you know how strong they are.

— Mrs. Miracle

"Sugar cookies," Jake said to himself. A rush of memories warmed him. Memories of his mother and sister at Christmas. Spicy scents in the air — cinnamon and ginger and cloves. Those sensory memories had been so deeply buried, he'd all but forgotten them.

"We sold three of the SuperRobots this afternoon," Mrs. Miracle said, breaking into his thoughts.

Just three? Jake felt a sense of dread. He'd need to sell a lot more than three a day to unload the five hundred robots he'd ordered. He checked the computer, which instantly gave him the total number sold since Black Friday. When he saw the screen, his heart sank down to his shoes. This wasn't good. Not good at all. Jake had made a bold decision, hoping to prove himself to his father, and he was about to fall flat on his face.

"I'll be leaving for the night," Mrs. Miracle announced. "Karen —" the other sales associate "— is already gone."

He glanced at his watch. Five after nine. "By all means. You've put in a full day."

"So have you."

As the owner's son, Jake was expected to stay late. He wouldn't ask anything of his staff that he wasn't willing to do himself. That had been drilled into him by his father, who lived by the same rules.

"It's a lovely night for a walk in the park, don't you think?" the older woman said wistfully.

Jake lived directly across from Central Park. He often jogged through the grounds during the summer months, but winter was a different story.

Mrs. Miracle patted him on the back. "I appreciate that you let me stay here in the toy department," she said.

Jake turned to look at her. He hadn't said anything to the older woman about getting her transferred. He couldn't imagine HR had, either. He wondered how she'd found out about his sudden decision to keep her with him. Actually, it'd been Holly's comment about having a grandmotherly figure around that had influenced him. That, and Emily's obvious rapport with children.

"Good night, Mrs. Miracle," he said.

"Good night, Mr. Finley. Oh, and I don't think you need to worry about that robot," she said. "It's going to do very well. Mark my words."

Now it appeared the woman was a mind reader, too.

"I hope you're right," he murmured.

"I am," she said, reaching for her purse. "And remember, this is a lovely evening for a stroll through the park. It's an excellent way to clear your head of worries."

Again, she'd caught him unawares. Jake had no idea he could be so easily read. Good thing he didn't play high-stakes poker. That thought amused him as he finished up for the day and left the store.

He was grateful not to run into his father because J.R. would certainly question him about those robots. No doubt his father already knew the dismal truth; the click of a computer key would show him everything.

When Jake reached his apartment, he was hungry and restless. He unwrapped the plate of cookies and quickly ate two. If this

74

wasn't his mother's recipe, then it was a very similar one. They tasted the same as the cookies he recalled from his childhood.

Standing by the picture window that overlooked the park, he remembered the Christmas his mother and sister had been killed. The shock and pain of it seemed as fresh now as it'd been all those years ago. No wonder his father still refused to celebrate the holiday. Jake couldn't, either.

When he looked out, he noticed how brightly lit the park was. Horse-drawn carriages clattered past, and although he couldn't hear the clopping of the horses' hooves, it sounded in his mind as clearly as if he'd been out on the street. He suddenly saw himself with his parents and his sister, all huddled under a blanket in a carriage. The horse had been named Silver, he remembered, and the snow had drifted softly down. That was almost twenty-one years ago, the winter they'd died, and he hadn't taken a carriage ride since.

Mrs. Miracle had suggested he go for a walk that evening. An odd idea, he thought, especially after a long day spent dealing with harried shoppers. The last thing he'd normally want to do was spend even more time on his feet. And yet he felt irresistibly attracted to the park. The cheerful lights, the

75

elegant carriages, the man on the corner selling roasted chestnuts, drew him like a kid to a Christmas tree.

None of this made any sense. He was exhausted, doubting himself and his judgment, entangled in memories he'd rather ignore. Perhaps a swift walk would chase away the demons that hounded him.

Putting on his coat, he wrapped the cashmere scarf around his neck. George, the building doorman, opened the front door and, hunching his shoulders against the wind, Jake hurried across the street.

"Aunt Holly, can we buy hot chestnuts?"

The young boy's voice immediately caught Jake's attention. He turned abruptly and came face-to-face with Holly Larson. The fourth time in less than twenty-four hours.

"Jake!"

"Holly."

They stared at each other, both apparently too shocked to speak.

She found her voice first. "What are you doing here?"

He pointed to the apartment building on the other side of the street. "I live over there. What are you doing here this late?"

"How late *is* it?"

He checked his watch. "Twenty to ten."

"Ten!" she cried. "You've got to be kidding. I had no idea it was so late. Hurry up, Gabe, it's time we got to the subway."

"Can we buy some chestnuts first?" he asked, gazing longingly at the vendor's cart.

"Not now. Come on, we have to go."

"I've never had roasted chestnuts before," the boy complained.

"Neither have I," Jake said, although that wasn't strictly true, and stepped up to the vendor. "Three, please."

"Jake, you shouldn't."

"Oh, come on, it'll be fun." He paid for the chestnuts, then handed bags to Holly and Gabe.

"I'm not sure how we got this far north," Holly said, walking close to his side as the three of them strolled down the street, eating chestnuts. "Gabe wanted to see the carriages in the park."

"Lindy told me about them." Gabe spoke with his mouth full. "Lindy Lee."

"Lindy Lee's my boss," Holly explained. "The designer."

Jake knew who she was, impressed that Holly worked for such a respected industry name.

"We went into Holly's office to decorate for Christmas, and Lindy was there and she let me put up stuff around her desk. That's when she told me about the horses in the

77

park," Gabe said.

"Did you go for a ride?" Jake asked.

Gabe shook his head sadly. "Aunt Holly said it costs a lot of money."

"It is expensive," Jake agreed. "But sometimes you can make a deal with the driver. Do you want me to try?"

"Yeah!" Gabe said excitedly. "I've never been in a carriage before — not even once."

"Jake, no," Holly whispered, and laid a restraining hand on his arm. "I should get him home and in bed."

"Aunt Holly, *please!*" The eight-year-old's plaintive cry rang out. "It's Saturday."

"You're turning down a carriage ride?" Jake asked. He saw the dreamy look that came over Holly as a carriage rolled past — a white carriage drawn by a midnight-black horse. "Have you ever been on one?"

"No . . ."

"Then that settles it. The three of us are going." Several carriages had lined up along the street. Jake walked over to the first one and asked his price, which he willingly paid. All that talk about negotiating had been just that — talk. This was the perfect end to a magical day. Magical because of a plate of silly sugar cookies. Magical because of Holly and Gabe. Magical because of Christmas, reluctant though he was to admit it.

He helped Holly up into the carriage. When she was seated, he lifted Gabe so the boy could climb aboard, too. Finally he hoisted himself onto the bench across from Holly and Gabe. They shared a thick fuzzy blanket.

"This is great," Gabe exclaimed. "I can hardly wait to tell my dad."

Holly smiled delightedly. "I'm surprised he's still awake," she said. "We've been on the go for hours."

"There's nothing like seeing Christmas through the eyes of a child, is there?"

"Nothing."

"Reminds me of when I was a kid . . ."

The carriage moved into Central Park and, even at this hour, the place was alive with activity.

"Oh, look, Gabe," Holly said, pointing at the carousel. She wrapped her arm around the boy, who snuggled closer. "We'll go on the carousel this spring."

He nodded sleepily. The ride lasted about thirty minutes, and by the time they returned to the park entrance, Gabe's eyes had drifted shut.

"I was afraid this would happen," Holly whispered.

"We'll go to my apartment, and I'll contact a car service to get you home."

Holly shook her head. "I . . . appreciate that, but we'll take the subway."

"Nonsense," Jake said.

"Jake, I can't afford a car service."

"It's on me."

"No." She shook her head again. "I can't let you do that."

"You can and you will. If I hadn't insisted on the carriage ride, you'd have been home by now."

She looked as if she wanted to argue more but changed her mind. "Then I'll graciously accept and say thank-you. It's been a magical evening."

Magical. The same word he'd used himself. He leaped down, helped her and Gabe out, then carried Gabe across the street. The doorman held the door for them.

"Evening, Mr. Finley."

"Evening, George."

Holly followed him onto the elevator. When they reached the tenth floor and the doors glided open, he led the way down the hall to his apartment. He had to shift the boy in his arms to get his key in the lock.

Once inside Holly looked around her, eyes wide. By New York standards, his apartment was huge. His father had lived in it for fifteen years before moving to a different place. This apartment had suited Jake, so he'd taken it over.

"I see you're like me. I haven't had time to decorate for Christmas, either," she finally said. "I was so late getting the office done that I had to come in on a Saturday to do it."

"I don't decorate for the holidays," he said without explaining the reasons. He knew he probably sounded a little brusque; he hadn't meant to.

"I suppose you get enough of that working for the store."

He nodded, again avoiding an explanation. He laid a sleeping Gabe on the sofa.

"I'll see how long we'll have to wait for a car," he said. The number was on speed dial; he used it often, since he didn't own a car himself. In midtown Manhattan car ownership could be more of a liability than a benefit. He watched Holly walk over to the picture window and gaze outside. Apparently she found the scene as mesmerizing as he had earlier. Although he made every effort to ignore Christmas, it stared back at him from the street, the city, the park. New York was always intensely alive but never more so than in December.

The call connected with the dispatcher. "How may I help you?"

Jake identified himself and gave his account number and address, and was assured a car would be there in fifteen minutes.

"I'll ride with you," Jake told her when he'd hung up the phone.

His offer appeared to surprise her. "You don't need to do that."

"True, but I'd like to," he said with a smile.

She smiled shyly back. "I'd like it, too." Walking away from the window, she sighed. "I don't understand why, but I feel like I've known you for ages."

"I feel the same way."

"Was it only yesterday morning that you paid for my latte?"

"You were a damsel in distress."

"And you were my knight in shining armor," she said warmly. "You're still in character this evening."

He sensed that she wanted to change the subject because she turned away from him, resting her gaze on something across the room. "You know, you have the ideal spot for a Christmas tree in that corner," she said.

"I haven't celebrated Christmas in more than twenty years," Jake blurted out, shocking himself even more than Holly.

"I beg your pardon?"

Jake went back into the kitchen and found

that his throat had gone dry and his hands sweaty. He never talked about his mother and sister. Not with anyone. Including his father.

"You don't believe in Christmas?" she asked, trailing after him. "What about Hanukkah?"

"Neither." He'd dug himself into a hole and the only way out was to explain. "My mother and sister were killed on Christmas Eve twenty-one years ago. A freak car accident that happened in the middle of a snowstorm, when two taxis collided."

"Oh, Jake. I'm so sorry."

"Dad and I agreed to forget about Christmas from that point forward."

Holly moved to his side. She didn't say a word and he was grateful. When people learned of the tragedy — almost always from someone other than him — they rarely knew what to say or how to react. It was an uncomfortable situation and still painful; he usually mumbled some remark about how long ago the accident had been and then tried to put it out of his mind. But he *couldn't,* any more than his father could.

Holly slid her arms around him and simply laid her head against his chest. For a moment, Jake stood unmoving as she held him. Then he placed his own arms around her. It felt as though she was an anchor, securing him in an unsteady sea. He needed her. *Wanted* her. Before he fully realized what he was doing, he lifted her head and lowered his mouth to hers.

The kiss was filled with urgency and need. She slipped her arms around his neck, and her touch had a powerful effect on him.

He tangled his fingers in her dark shoulder-length hair and brought his mouth to hers a second time. Soon they were so involved in each other that it took him far longer than it should to hear the ringing of his phone.

He broke away in order to answer; as he suspected, the car was downstairs, waiting. When he told Holly, she immediately put on her coat. Gabe continued to sleep as Jake scooped him up, holding the boy carefully in both arms.

George opened the lobby door for them. Holly slid into the vehicle first, and then as Jake started to hand her the boy, he noticed a movement on the other side of the street.

"Jake?" Holly called from the car. "Please, there's no need for you to come. You've been so kind already."

"I want to see you safely home," he said as he stared across the street. For just an instant — it must have been his imagination

— he was sure he'd seen Emily Merkle, better known as Mrs. Miracle.

Six

Forbidden fruit creates many jams.
— Mrs. Miracle

The phone rang just as Holly and Gabe walked into the apartment after church the next morning. For one wild second Holly thought it might be Jake.

Or rather, *hoped* it was Jake.

Although she'd been dead on her feet by the time they got to Brooklyn, she couldn't sleep. She'd lain awake for hours, thinking about the kisses they'd shared, replaying every minute of their time together. All of this was so unexpected and yet so welcome. Jake was —

"Hello," she said, sounding breathless with anticipation.

"What's this I hear about you turning my son into a girl?"

"Mickey!" Her brother's voice was as clear as if he were in the next room. He tried to

86

phone on a regular basis, but it wasn't easy. The most reliable form of communication had proved to be email.

"So you're baking cookies with my son, are you?" he teased.

"We had a blast." Gabe was leaping up and down, eager to speak to his father. "Here, I'll let Gabe tell you about it himself." She passed the phone to her nephew, who immediately grabbed it.

"Dad! Dad, guess what? I went to Aunt Holly's office to help her decorate and then she took me to see the big tree at Rockefeller Center and we watched the skaters and had hot chocolate and then we walked to Central Park and had hot dogs for dinner, and, oh, we went to see Mrs. Miracle. I helped Aunt Holly roll out cookies and . . ." He paused for breath.

Evidently Mickey took the opportunity to ask a few questions, because Gabe nodded a couple of times.

"Mrs. Miracle is the lady in the toy department at Finley's," he said.

He was silent for a few seconds.

"She's really nice," Gabe continued. "She reminds me of Grandma Larson. I gave her a plate of cookies, and Aunt Holly gave cookies to Jake." Silence again, followed by "He's Aunt Holly's new boyfriend and he's really, really nice."

"Maybe I should talk to your father now," Holly inserted, wishing Gabe hadn't been so quick to mention Jake's name.

Gabe clutched the receiver in both hands and turned his back, unwilling to relinquish the phone.

"Jake took us on a carriage ride in Central Park and then . . ." Gabe stopped talking for a few seconds. "I don't know what happened after that 'cause I fell asleep."

Mickey was asking something else, and although Holly strained to hear what it was, she couldn't.

Whatever his question, Gabe responded by glancing at Holly, grinning widely and saying, "Oh, yeah."

"Are you two talking about me?" she demanded, half laughing and half annoyed.

She was ignored. Apparently Gabe felt there was a lot to tell his father, because he cupped his hand around the mouthpiece and whispered loudly, "I think they *kissed.*"

"Gabe!" she protested. If she wanted her brother to know this, she'd tell him herself.

"Okay," Gabe said, nodding. He held out the phone to her. "Dad wants to talk to you."

Holly took it from him and glared down at her nephew.

"So I hear you've found a new love interest," Mickey said in the same tone he'd used to tease her when they were teenagers.

"Oh, stop. Jake and I hardly know each other."

"How'd you meet?"

"At Starbucks. Mickey, please, it's nothing. I only met him on Friday." It felt longer than two days, but this was far too soon to even suggest they were in a relationship.

"Gabe doesn't seem to feel that's a problem."

"Okay, so I took Jake a plate of cookies like Gabe said — it was just a thank-you for buying me a coffee — and . . . and we happened to run into him last evening in Central Park. It's no big deal. He's a nice person and, well . . . like I said, we've just met."

"But it looks promising," her brother added.

Holly hated to acknowledge how true that was. Joy and anticipation had surged through her from the moment she and Jake kissed. Still, she was afraid to admit this to her brother — and, for that matter, afraid to admit it to herself. "It's too soon to say that yet."

"Ah, so you're still hung up on Bill?"

Was she? Holly didn't think so. If Bill had

ended the relationship by telling her the chemistry just wasn't there, she could've accepted that. Instead, he'd left her with serious doubts regarding her parenting abilities.

"Is that it?" Mickey pressed.

"No," she said. "Not at all. Bill and I weren't really meant to be together. I think we both realized that early on, only neither of us was ready to be honest about it."

"Mmm." Mickey made a sound of agreement. "Things are going better with Gabe, aren't they?"

"Much better."

"Good."

"He's adjusting and so am I." This past week seemed to have been a turning point. They were more at ease with each other. Gabe had made new friends and was getting used to life without his father — and with her. She knew she insisted on rules Mickey didn't bother with — like making their beds every morning, drinking milk with breakfast and, of course, putting the toilet seat down. But Gabe hardly complained at all anymore.

"What was it he told Santa he wanted for Christmas?" Mickey asked.

"So he emailed you about the visit with Santa, did he?"

"Yup, he sent the email right after he got home. He seemed quite excited."

"It's Intellytron the SuperRobot."

At her reference to the toy, Gabe's eyes lit up and he nodded vigorously.

"We found them in Finley's Department Store. Mrs. Miracle, the woman Gabe mentioned, works there . . . and Jake does, too."

"Didn't Gabe tell me Jake's name is Finley?" Mickey asked. "He said he heard Mrs. Miracle call him that — Mr. Finley. Is he related to the guy who owns the store?"

"Y-e-s." How dense could she be? Holly felt like slapping her forehead. She'd known his name was Finley from the beginning and it hadn't meant a thing to her. But now . . . now she realized Jake was probably related to the Finley family — was possibly even the owner's son. No wonder he could afford to live where he did. He hadn't given the price of the carriage ride or the car service a second thought, either.

She had the sudden, awful feeling that she was swimming in treacherous waters and there wasn't a life preserver in sight.

"Holly?"

"I . . . I think he must be." She'd been so caught up in her juvenile fantasies, based on the coincidence of their meetings, that she hadn't paid attention to anything else.

"You sound like this is shocking news."

"I hadn't put two and two together," she confessed.

"And now you're scared."

"I guess I am."

"Don't be. He puts his pants on one leg at a time like everyone else, if you'll pardon the cliché. He's just a guy."

"Right."

"You don't seem too sure of that."

Holly wasn't. A chill had overtaken her and she hugged herself with one arm. "I need to think about this."

"While you're thinking, tell me more about this robot that's got my son so excited."

"It's expensive."

"How . . . expensive?"

Holly heard the hesitation in her brother's voice. He had his own financial problems. "Don't worry — I've got it. This is on me."

"You're sure about that?"

"Positive." The Christmas bonus checks were due the following Friday. If all went well, hers should cover the price of the toy with enough left over for a really special Christmas dinner.

Christmas.

When she woke that morning, still warm

under the covers, Holly's first thought had been of Jake. She'd had the craziest idea that . . . well, it was out of the question now.

What Jake had confided about his mother and sister had nearly broken her heart. The tragedy had not only robbed him of his mother and sibling, it had destroyed his pleasure in Christmas. Holly had hoped to change that, but the mere notion seemed ridiculous now. She'd actually planned to invite Jake to spend Christmas Day with her and Gabe. She knew now that he'd never accept. He was a Finley, after all, a man whose background was vastly different from her own.

Half-asleep, she'd pictured the three of them sitting around her table, a lovely golden-brown turkey with sage stuffing resting in the center. She'd imagined Christmas music playing and the tree lights blinking merrily, enhancing the celebratory mood. She couldn't believe she'd even considered such a thing, knowing what she did now.

"I have a Christmas surprise coming your way," Mickey said. "I'm just hoping it arrives in time for the holidays."

"It doesn't matter," she assured her brother, dragging her thoughts away from Jake. She focused on her brother and nephew — which was exactly what she intended to do from this point forward. She needed to forget this romantic fantasy she'd invented within a day of meeting Jake Finley.

"I can guarantee Gabe will like it and so will you," Mickey was saying.

Holly couldn't begin to guess what Mickey might have purchased in Afghanistan for Christmas, but then her brother had always been full of surprises. He'd probably ordered something over the internet, she decided.

"Mom and Dad mailed us a package, as well," she told him. "The box got here this week."

"From Haiti? What would they be sending?"

"I don't have a clue," she said. Once the tree was up she'd arrange the gifts underneath it.

"You're going to wait until Christmas morning, aren't you?" he asked. "Don't open anything before that."

"Of course we'll wait." Even as kids, they'd managed not to peek at their gifts.

Mickey laughed, then grew serious. "This won't be an ordinary Christmas, will it?"

Holly hadn't dwelled on not being with her parents. Her father, a retired dentist, and her mother, a retired nurse, had offered their services in a health clinic for twelve months after the devastating earthquake. They'd been happy about the idea of giving back, and Holly had been happy for them. This Christmas was supposed to be Mickey, Gabe and her for the holidays — and then Mickey's National Guard unit had been called up and he'd left to serve his country.

"It could be worse," she said, and her thoughts involuntarily went to Jake and his father, who refused to celebrate Christmas at all.

"Next year everything will be different," Mickey told her.

"Yes, it will," she agreed.

Her brother spoke to Gabe for a few more minutes and then said goodbye. Gabe was pensive after the conversation with his father and so was Holly, but for different reasons.

"How about toasted cheese sandwiches and tomato soup for lunch?" she suggested, hoping to lighten the mood. "That was your dad's and my favorite Sunday lunch when we were growing up."

Gabe looked at her suspiciously. "What kind of cheese?"

Holly shrugged. "Regular cheese?" By that she meant the plastic-wrapped slices, Gabe's idea of cheese.

"You won't use any of that buffalo stuff, will you?"

She grinned. "Buffalo mozzarella. Nope, this is plain old sliced regular cheese in a package."

"Okay, as long as the soup comes from a can. That's the way Dad made it and that's how I like it."

"You got it," she said, and moved into the kitchen.

Gabe sat on a stool and watched her work, leaning his elbows on the kitchen counter. Holly wasn't fooled by his intent expression. He wasn't interested in spending time with her; he was keeping a close eye on their lunch in case she tried to slip in a foreign ingredient. After a moment he released a deep sigh.

"What's that about?" she asked.

"I miss my dad."

"I know you do, sweetheart. I miss him, too."

"And Grandma and Grandpa."

"And they miss us."

Gabe nodded. "It's not so bad living with you. I thought it was at first, but you're okay."

"Thanks." She hid a smile and set a piece of buttered bread on the heated griddle, then carefully placed a slice of processed cheese on top before adding the second piece of bread. She planned to have a plain cheese sandwich herself — one with *real* cheese.

Obviously satisfied that she was preparing his lunch according to his specifications, Gabe clambered off the stool. "Can we go to the movies this afternoon?"

"Maybe." She had to be careful with her entertainment budget, especially since there were additional expenses coming up this month. "It might be better if we got a video."

"Can I invite a friend over?"

She hesitated a moment, afraid he might want to ask his new friend, Billy.

"Sure," she said. "How about Jonathan Krantz?" Jonathan was another eight-year-old who lived in the building, and Caroline, his mother, sometimes babysat for her.

That was acceptable to Gabe.

After lunch they walked down to the neighborhood video store, found a movie they could both agree on and then asked Jonathan to join them.

Holly did her best to pay attention to the movie; however, her mind had a will of its own. No matter how hard she tried, all she could think about was Jake. He didn't phone and that was just as well. She wasn't sure what she would've said if he had.

Then again, he hadn't asked for her phone number. Still, he could get it easily enough if he wanted. . . .

Late Sunday night, after Gabe was asleep, Holly went on the computer and did a bit of research. Sure enough, Jake was related to the owner. Not only that, he was the son and heir.

Monday morning, Holly dropped Gabe off at school and took the subway into Manhattan. As she walked past Starbucks, she felt a twinge of longing — for more than just the coffee they served. This was where she'd met Jake. Jake Finley.

As she walked briskly past Starbucks, the door flew open and Jake Finley dashed out, calling her name.

Holly pretended not to hear.

"Holly!" he shouted, running after her. "Wait up!"

SEVEN

Coincidence is when God chooses to
remain anonymous.
— Mrs. Miracle

"Wait up!" Jake called. Holly acted as if she
hadn't heard him. Jake knew better. She was
clearly upset about something, although he
couldn't figure out what. His mind raced
with possibilities, but he couldn't come up
with a single one that made sense.

Finally she turned around.

Jake relaxed. Just seeing her again brought
him a feeling of happiness he couldn't
define. He barely knew Holly Larson, yet
he hadn't been able to forget her. She was
constantly in his thoughts, constantly with
him, and perhaps the most puzzling of all
was the *rightness* he felt in her presence. He
couldn't think of any other way to describe
it.

Jake had resisted the urge to contact her

on Sunday, afraid of coming on too strong. They'd seen quite a bit of each other in the past few days, seemingly thrown together by fate. Coincidence? He supposed so, and yet . . . It was as though a providential hand was behind all this. Admittedly that sounded fanciful, even melodramatic. Nevertheless, four chance meetings in quick succession was hard to explain.

With someone else, a different kind of woman, Jake might have suspected these meetings had been contrived, and certainly this morning's was pure manipulation on his part. He'd hoped to run into her casually. But he hadn't expected to see Holly walk directly past the coffee shop. He couldn't allow this opportunity to pass.

She looked up at him expectantly; she didn't say anything.

"Good morning," he said, unsure of her mood.

"Hi." She just missed making eye contact.

He felt her reluctance and frowned, unable to fathom what he might have done to upset her. "What's wrong?" he asked.

"Nothing."

"Then why won't you look at me?"

The question forced her to raise her eyes and meet his. She held his gaze for only a fraction of a second before glancing away.

The traffic light changed and, side by side, they crossed the street.

"I'd like to take you to dinner," he said. He'd decided that if he invited her out on a real date they could straighten out the problem, whatever it was.

"When?"

At least she hadn't turned him down flat. That was encouraging. "Whenever you say." He'd rearrange his schedule if necessary. "Tonight? Tomorrow? I'm free every evening. Or I can be." He wanted it understood that he wasn't involved with anyone else. In fact, he hadn't been in a serious relationship in years.

His primary goal for the past decade had been to learn the retail business from the ground up, and as a result his social life had suffered. He worked long hours and that had taken a toll on his relationships. After his last breakup, which was in . . . Jake had to stop and think. June, he remembered. Had it really been that long? At any rate, Judith had told him it was over before they'd really begun.

At the time he'd felt bad, but agreed it was probably for the best. Funny how easily he could let go of a woman with hardly a pause after just four weeks. Judith had been attractive, successful, intelligent, but there'd been no real connection between them. The thought of letting Holly walk out of his life was a completely different scenario, one that filled him with dread.

All he could think about on Sunday was when he'd see her again. His pride had influenced his decision not to call her; he didn't want her to know how important she'd become to him in such a short time. Despite that, he'd gone to Starbucks first thing this morning.

"Tonight?" she repeated, referring to his dinner invitation. "You mean this evening?"

"Sure," he said with a shrug. "I'm available Tuesday night if that's better for you."

She hesitated, as if considering his offer. "Thanks, but I don't have anyone to look after Gabe."

"I could bring us dinner." He wasn't willing to give up that quickly.

Her eyes narrowed. "Why are you trying so hard?"

"Why are you inventing excuses not to see me?"

He didn't understand her reluctance. Saturday, when he'd dropped her off at her Brooklyn apartment and kissed her goodnight, she'd practically melted in his arms. Now she couldn't get away from him fast enough.

Holly stared down at the sidewalk. People hurried past them and around them. They stood like boulders in the middle of a fast-moving stream, neither of them moving, neither talking.

"I . . . I didn't know who you were," she eventually admitted. "Not until later."

"I told you my name's Jake Finley." He didn't pretend not to understand what she meant. This wasn't the first time his family name had intimidated someone. He just hadn't expected that sort of reaction from Holly. He'd assumed she knew, and that was part of her charm because it hadn't mattered to her.

"I know you did," she countered swiftly. "And I feel stupid for not connecting the dots."

He stiffened. "And my name bothers you?"

"Not really," she said, and her gaze locked with his before she slowly lowered her lashes. "I guess it does, but not for the reasons you're assuming."

"What exactly am I assuming?" he asked.

"That I'd use you."

"For what?" he demanded.

"Well, for one thing, that robot toy. We both know how badly Gabe wants it for Christmas and it's expensive and you might think I . . ."

"*What* would I think?" he asked forcefully when she didn't complete her sentence.

"That I'd want you to get me the toy."

"Would you ask me to do that?" If she did, he'd gladly purchase it — retail price — on her behalf.

"No. Never." Her eyes flared with the intensity of her response. She started to leave and Jake followed.

"Then it's a moot point." He began to walk, carefully matching his longer stride to her shorter one. "Under no circumstances will I purchase that toy for you. Agreed?"

"Agreed," she said.

"Anything else?"

Holly looked at him and then away. "I don't come from a powerful family or know famous people or —"

"Do you think I care?"

"No, but if you did, you'd be plain out of luck."

He smiled. "That's fine with me."

"Okay," she said, stopping abruptly. "Can you explain why you want to see me?"

Jake wished he had a logical response. He felt drawn to her in ways he hadn't with other women. "I can't say for sure, but deep down I feel that if we were to walk away from each other right now, I'd regret it."

"You do?" she asked softly, and pressed her hand to her heart. "Jake, I feel the same way. What's happening to us?"

He didn't have an answer. "I don't know." But he definitely felt it, and that feeling intensified with each meeting.

They started walking again. "So, can I see you tonight?" he asked. That was important, necessary.

Her face fell. "I wasn't making it up, about not having anyone to take care of Gabe. If you were serious about bringing us dinner . . ."

"I was."

Her face brightened. "Then that would work out perfectly."

"Do you like take-out Chinese?" he asked, thinking Gabe would enjoy it, as well.

"Love it."

"Me, too, but you'll have to use chopsticks."

"Okay, I'll give it a try."

"Great." Jake breathed easier. Everything was falling into place, just the way he'd hoped it would. He glanced at his watch and grimaced. He was late for work. He hoped Karen or Mrs. Miracle had covered for him.

Retreating now, taking two steps backward, he called out to Holly, "Six-thirty? At your place?"

She nodded eagerly. "Yes. And thank you, Jake, thank you so much."

He raised his hand. "See you tonight."

"Tonight," she echoed, and they both turned and hurried off to their respective jobs.

Jake's step was noticeably lighter as he rushed toward the department store. By the time he arrived, ten minutes later than usual, he was breathless. He'd just clocked in and headed for the elevator when his father stopped him, wearing a frown that told him J.R. wasn't happy.

"Are you keeping bankers' hours these days?"

"No," Jake told him. "I had an appointment." A slight stretch of the truth.

"I was looking for you."

"Any particular reason?" Jake asked. He'd bet his lunch break this sudden interest in the toy department had to do with those robots.

His father surprised him, however, with a completely different question. "I heard from HR that you requested a transfer for one of the seasonal staff. . . ."

"Mrs. Miracle."

"Who? No, that wasn't the name."

"No, it's Merkle or Michaels or something

like that. The name badge mistakenly says Miracle, and she insisted that's what we call her."

His father seemed confused, which was fine with Jake. He felt he was being rather clever to keep J.R.'s attention away from the robots.

J.R. ignored the comment. "You asked for this Mrs. Miracle or whoever she is to be transferred and then you changed your mind. Do I understand correctly?"

"Yes. After I made the initial request, I realized she was a good fit for the department — a grandmotherly figure who relates well to kids *and* parents. She adds exactly the right touch."

"I see," his father murmured. "Okay, whatever you decide is fine."

That was generous, seeing that *he* was the department head, Jake mused with more affection than sarcasm.

"While I have you, tell me, how are sales of that expensive robot going?"

Jake wasn't fooled. His father already knew the answer to that. "Sales are picking up. We sold a total of twenty-five over the weekend."

"Twenty-five," his father said slowly. "There're still a lot of robots left in the storeroom, though, aren't there?"

"Yes," Jake admitted.

"That's what I thought."

He made some additional remark Jake couldn't quite grasp, but it didn't sound like something he wanted to hear, anyway, so he didn't ask J.R. to repeat it.

As he entered the toy department, clipping on his "Manager" badge, Jake was glad to see Mrs. Miracle on duty.

"Good morning, Mr. Finley," she said, looking pleased with herself.

"Good morning. I apologize for being late —"

"No problem. I sold two Intellytrons this morning."

"Already?" This was encouraging news and improved his workday almost before it had started. "That's wonderful!"

"They seem to be catching on."

The phone rang just then, and Jake stepped behind the counter to answer. The woman at the other end of the line was looking for Intellytron and sighed with audible relief when Jake assured her he had plenty in stock. She asked that he hold one for her.

"I'll be happy to," Jake said. He found Mrs. Miracle watching him, smiling, when he ended the conversation. "I think you might be right," he said. "That was a woman calling about Intellytron. She sounded excited when I told her we've got them."

Mrs. Miracle rubbed her palms together. "I knew it." The morning lull was about to end; in another half hour, the store would explode with customers. Since toys were on the third floor, it took time for shoppers to drift up the escalators and elevators, so they still had a few minutes of relative peace. Jake decided to take advantage of it by questioning his rather unusual employee.

"I thought I saw you on Saturday night," he commented in a nonchalant voice, watching her closely.

"Me?" she asked.

Jake noted that she looked a bit sheepish. "Did you happen to take a walk around Central Park around ten or ten-thirty?"

"My heavens, no! After spending all day on my feet, the last thing I'd do is wander aimlessly around Central Park. At that time of night, no less." Her expression turned serious. "What makes you ask?"

"I could've sworn that was you I saw across from the park."

She laughed as though the question was ludicrous. "You're joking, aren't you?"

"No." Jake grew even more suspicious. Her nervous reaction seemed to imply that she wasn't being completely truthful. "Don't you remember? You suggested I take a stroll

109

through the park."

"I said that?"

"You did," he insisted. He wasn't about to be dismissed quite this easily. "You said it would help clear my head."

"After a long day at work? My goodness, what was I thinking?"

Jake figured the question was rhetorical, so he didn't respond. "I met Holly Larson and her nephew there," he told her.

"My, that was a nice coincidence, wasn't it?"

"Very nice," he agreed.

"Are you seeing her again?" the older woman asked.

"Yes, as a matter of fact, I am." He didn't share any details. The less she knew about his personal life, the better. Mrs. Miracle might appear to be an innocent senior citizen, but he had his doubts. Not that he suspected anything underhanded or nefarious. She seemed . . . Jake couldn't come up with the right word. He liked Mrs. Miracle and she was an excellent employee, a natural saleswoman. And yet . . . He didn't really know much about her.

And what he did know didn't seem to add up.

EIGHT

Aspire to inspire before you expire.
— Mrs. Miracle

Holly felt as if she was walking on air the rest of the way into the office. It didn't matter how rotten her day turned out to be; no one was going to ruin it after her conversation with Jake.

She'd spent a miserable Sunday and had worked herself into a state after she'd discovered Jake's position with the department store. Son and heir. Now, having talked to him, she realized her concerns were irrelevant. Okay, so his family was rich and influential; that didn't define him or say anything about the person he really was.

The question that, inevitably, kept going around and around in her mind was why someone like Jake Finley would be interested in *her*. The reality was that he could have his pick of women. To further complicate the situation, she was taking care of Gabe. Lots of men would see her nephew as an encumbrance. Apparently not Jake.

Holly was happy they'd gotten this settled. She felt reassured about his interest — and about the fact that he'd promised not to purchase the robot for her. Mickey had offered, too, but she knew he was financially strapped. Besides, getting Gabe this toy for Christmas — as *her* gift to him — was important to Holly.

She couldn't entirely explain why. Maybe because of Bill's implication that she wasn't good with kids. She had something to prove — if not to Bill or Mickey or even Jake, she had to prove it to herself. Nothing was going to keep her from making this the best possible Christmas for Gabe.

Holly entered her cubicle outside Lindy Lee's office and hung up her coat. She'd been surprised to find her boss in the office on Saturday afternoon and had tried to keep Gabe occupied so he wouldn't pester her. Unfortunately, Holly's efforts hadn't worked. She'd caught Gabe with Lindy Lee twice. One look made her suspect Lindy didn't really appreciate the intrusion. As soon as they'd finished putting up the decorations, Holly had dragged Gabe out with her. But this morning, as she looked around the office, she was pleased with her work. The bright red bulbs that hung outside her cubicle created an air of festivity. She couldn't help it — she started singing "Jingle Bells."

"Where is that file?" Lindy Lee shouted. She was obviously in her usual Monday-morning bad mood. Her employer was sorting through her in-basket, cursing impatiently under her breath.

Of course, Lindy Lee didn't mention *which* file she needed. But deciphering vague demands was all part and parcel of Holly's job. And fortunately she had a pretty good idea which one her boss required.

Walking into Lindy Lee's office, Holly reached across the top of the desk, picked up a file and handed it to her.

Lindy Lee growled something back, opened the file and then smiled. "Thank you."

"You're welcome," Holly said cheerfully.

The designer eyed her suspiciously. "What are *you* so happy about?" she asked.

"Nothing . . . I met up with a friend this morning, that's all."

"I take it this *friend* is a man."

Holly nodded. "A very special man."

"Honey, don't believe it." She laughed as though to say Holly had a lot to learn about the opposite sex. "Men will break your heart before breakfast and flush it down the toilet just for fun."

Holly didn't bother to explain about Jake. Lindy Lee's experience with men might be far more extensive than her own, but it was obviously different. Jake would never do anything to hurt her; she was sure of it. Besides, Lindy Lee socialized in different circles — Jake's circles, she realized with a start. Still, Holly couldn't make herself believe Jake was the kind of man who'd mislead her. Even though they'd known each other so briefly, every instinct she had told her she could trust him, and she did.

No irrational demand or bad temper was going to spoil her day, Holly decided. Because that evening she was seeing Jake.

Holly guessed wrong. Her day was ruined.

Early that afternoon she slipped back into her cubicle after delivering Lindy Lee's latest sketches to the tech department, where they'd be translated into patterns, which would then be sewn up as samples. Lindy was talking to the bookkeeper and apparently neither one noticed that she'd returned.

Holly hadn't intended to listen in on the conversation, but it would've been impossible not to with Lindy Lee's office door wide open. In Holly's opinion, if Lindy wanted to keep the conversation private, then it was up to her to close the door.

"Christmas bonuses are due this Friday," Marsha, the bookkeeper, reminded their boss.

"Due." Lindy Lee pounced on the word. "Since when is a bonus *due?* It's my understanding that a bonus is exactly that — a bonus — an extra that's distributed at my discretion."

"Well, yes, but you've given us one every year since you went out on your own."

"That's because I could afford to."

"You've had a decent year," Marsha said calmly.

Holly wanted to stand and cheer. Marsha was right; profits were steady despite the economy. The staff had worked hard, although their employer took them for granted. Lindy Lee didn't appear to notice or value the team who backed her both personally and professionally. More times than she cared to count, Holly had dropped off and picked up Lindy's dry cleaning or run errands for her. She often went above and beyond anything listed in her job description.

Not once had she complained. The way Holly figured it, her main task was to give

Lindy Lee the freedom to be creative and do what she did best and that was design clothes.

"A *decent* year, perhaps," Lindy Lee repeated. "But not a stellar one."

"True," Marsha agreed. "But you're holding your own in a terrible economy."

"All right, I'll reconsider." Lindy Lee walked over to the window, her back to Holly. Not wanting to be caught listening, Holly quietly stood. There was plenty to do away from her desk — like filing. Clutching a sheaf of documents, she held her breath as she waited for Lindy's decision.

"Everyone gets the same bonus as last year," Lindy Lee said with a beleaguered sigh.

Holly released her breath.

"Everyone except Holly Larson."

Her heart seemed to stop.

"Why not Holly?" Marsha asked.

"She doesn't deserve it," Lindy Lee said flippantly. "She's out of the office at the stroke of five and she's been late for work a number of mornings, as well."

The bookkeeper was quick to defend Holly. "Yes, but she's looking after her nephew while her brother's in Afghanistan. This hasn't been easy for her, you know."

Lindy Lee whirled around and Holly

moved from her line of vision in the nick of time. She flattened herself against the wall and continued to listen.

"Yes, yes, I met the boy this weekend. She brought him on Saturday when she came in to decorate."

"On her own time," Marsha said pointedly.

"True, but if she managed her time better, Holly could've done it earlier. As it is, the decorations are up much later than in previous years. If I was giving out bleeding-heart awards this Christmas, I'd make sure Holly got one. No, I won't change my mind," she snapped as Marsha began to protest. "A bonus is a bonus, and as far as I'm concerned Holly doesn't deserve one. It's about merit, you know, and going the extra mile, and she hasn't done that."

Holly gasped.

"But —"

"I've made my decision."

Marsha didn't argue further.

Holly didn't blame her. The bookkeeper had tried. Holly felt tears well up but blinked them away. She was a good employee; she worked hard. While Lindy Lee was correct — these days she *did* leave the office on time — there'd been many a night earlier in the year when she'd stayed late without being asked. She'd often gone that extra mile for her employer. Yet all Lindy seemed to remember was the past three months.

She felt sick to her stomach. So there'd be no bonus for her. Although the amount of money wasn't substantial — maybe five hundred dollars — it would've made all the difference. But somehow, she promised herself, she'd find a way to buy Gabe his special Christmas toy.

Even though she was distracted by her financial worries, Holly managed to enjoy dinner with Jake and Gabe that evening. Jake brought chopsticks along with their take-out Chinese — an order large enough to feed a family of eight. Several of the dishes were new to Holly. He'd chosen moo shu pork and shrimp in lobster sauce, plus barbecue pork, egg rolls, fried rice and almond fried chicken.

Gabe loved every minute of their time with Jake. As he so eloquently said, "It's nice being around a guy."

"I don't know," Jake commented as he slipped his arm around Holly's waist. "Women aren't so bad."

Gabe considered his comment carefully. "Aunt Holly's okay, I guess."

118

"You *guess*," she sputtered. Using her chopsticks she removed the last bit of almond fried chicken from her nephew's plate.

"Hey, that was mine," Gabe cried.

"That's what you get for criticizing women," Holly told him, and then, to prove her point, she reached for his fried dumpling, too. In retaliation, Gabe reached across for her egg roll, dropping it on the table.

Jake immediately retrieved it and stuck one end in his mouth. "Five-second rule," he said just before he bit down.

When they'd finished, they cleared the table and settled down in front of the television.

As Jake flipped through the channels, Gabe asked, "When are we gonna put up the Christmas tree?"

"This week," Holly told him. She'd need to budget carefully now that she wasn't going to get her bonus. The tree — she'd hoped to buy a real one — was an added expense she'd planned to cover with the extra money. This year she'd have to resort to the small artificial tree she'd stuck in the back of her coat closet.

The news that she wouldn't be receiving the bonus was devastating. Holly's first instinct had been to strike back. If everyone else was getting a bonus, it didn't seem fair that she wasn't. Still, Lindy Lee had a point. Holly hadn't been as dedicated to her job since Gabe came into her life. She had other responsibilities now.

That afternoon she'd toyed with the idea of looking for a new job. She could walk out — that would show Lindy Lee. Reason quickly asserted itself. She couldn't leave her job and survive financially. It could take her months to find a new one. And although this was an entry-level position, the chance to advance in the fashion world was an inducement she simply couldn't reject that easily. She'd made friends at the office, too. Friends like Marsha, who'd willingly defended her to their employer.

Besides, if she left her job, there'd be dozens who'd leap at the opportunity to take her place. No, Holly would swallow her disappointment and ride this out until Mickey returned. Next Christmas would be different.

"Can Jake help decorate the Christmas tree?" Gabe asked.

Jake was sitting next to her and Holly felt him tense. His face was pale, his expression shocked.

"Jake." Holly said his name softly and laid her hand on his forearm. "Are you okay?"

120

"Sure. Sorry, no decorating trees for me this year," he said in an offhand way.

"Why not?" Gabe pressed. "It's really fun. Aunt Holly said she'd make popcorn and we'd have cider. She has some ornaments from when she and my dad were kids. She won't let me see them until we put up the tree. It'll be lots of fun." His young face pleaded with Jake to reconsider.

Holly gently placed her hand on her nephew's shoulder. "Jake said another time," she reminded him. Jake hadn't participated in any of the usual Christmas traditions or activities in more than twenty years, ever since he'd lost his mother and sister.

"But there won't be another time," her nephew sulked. "I'll be with my dad next year."

"Jake's busy," Holly said, offering yet another excuse.

"Sorry to let you down, buddy," Jake told Gabe. "We'll do something else, all right?"

Gabe shrugged, his head hanging. "Okay."

"How about if I take you ice-skating at Rockefeller Center? Would you like that?"

"Wow!" In his excitement, Gabe propelled himself off the sofa and landed with a thud on the living room carpet. "I wanted to go skating last Saturday but Aunt Holly doesn't know how."

"She's a girl," Jake said in a stage whisper. Then he looked at her and grinned boyishly. "Frankly, I'm glad of it."

"As you should be," she returned under her breath.

"When can we go?" Gabe wasn't letting this opportunity slip through his fingers. He wanted to nail down the date as soon as possible. "I took skating lessons last winter," he said proudly.

Jake hesitated. "I'll need to get back to you once I see how everything goes at the store. It's the Christmas season, you know, so we might have to wait until the first week of the new year. How about Sunday the second?"

"That *long?*"

"Yes, but then I'll have more time to show you some classic moves. Deal?"

Gabe considered this compromise and finally nodded. "Deal." They clenched their fists and bumped them together to seal the bargain.

The three of them sat side by side and watched a rerun of *Everybody Loves Raymond* for the next half hour. Jake was beside her, his arm around her shoulders. Gabe sat to her left with his feet tucked beneath him.

When the program ended, Gabe turned

to Jake. "Do you want me to leave the room so you can kiss my aunt Holly?"

"Gabe!" Holly's cheeks were warm with embarrassment.

"What makes you suggest that?" Jake asked the boy.

Gabe stood in the center of the room. "My dad emailed and said if you came to the apartment, I should dis-discreetly leave for a few minutes, only I don't know what that word means. I think it means you want to kiss Aunt Holly without me watching. Right?"

Jake nodded solemnly. "Something like that."

"I thought so. Okay, I'm going to go and get ready for bed." He enunciated each word as if reading a line of dialogue from an unfamiliar play.

Jake winked at Holly. "Pucker up, sweetheart," he said, doing a recognizable imitation of Humphrey Bogart.

Holly rolled her eyes and clasped her hands prayerfully. "Ah, sweet romance."

As soon as the bedroom door closed, Jake pulled her into his arms. The kiss was everything she'd remembered and more. They kissed repeatedly until Gabe came back and stood in front of them. He cleared his throat.

"Should I go away again?" he asked.

"No, that's fine," Holly said. She had trouble speaking.

"Your timing is perfect," Jake assured the boy.

Jake left shortly after that, and once she'd let him out of the apartment, Holly leaned against the door, still a little breathless. Being with Jake was very nice, indeed, but she had something else on her mind at the moment — Intellytron the SuperRobot and how she was going to afford one before Christmas.

NINE

It's hard to stumble when you're
down on your knees.
— Shirley, Goodness and Mercy,
friends of Mrs. Miracle

Holly gave the situation regarding Gabe and the robot careful thought during the sleepless night that followed their dinner. She'd asked Jake about it when Gabe was out of earshot.

"There are still plenty left," he'd told her.

"But they're selling, aren't they?"

"Yes, sales are picking up."

That was good for him but unsettling for her. If she couldn't afford to pay for the robot until closer to Christmas, then she'd need to make a small deposit and put one on layaway now. She didn't know if Finley's offered that option; not many stores did anymore. She'd have to check with Jake. She dared not take a chance that Intellytron

125

would sell out before she had the cash.

While she was dead set against letting Jake purchase the robot for her, she hoped he'd be willing to put one aside, even if layaway wasn't a current practice at higher-end department stores. If she made their lunches, cut back on groceries and bought only what was absolutely necessary, she should be able to pay cash for the robot just before Christmas.

Tuesday morning she packed a hard-boiled egg and an apple for lunch. For Gabe she prepared a peanut butter and jelly sandwich, adding an apple for him, too, plus the last of the sugar cookies. Gabe hadn't been happy to take a packed lunch. He much preferred to buy his meal with his friends. But it was so much cheaper for him to bring it — and, at this point, necessary, although of course she couldn't tell him why. The leftover Chinese food figured into her money-saving calculations, too. It would make a great dinner.

On her lunch hour, after she'd eaten her apple and boiled egg, Holly hurried to Finley's to talk to Jake. She'd been uneasy from the moment she'd learned she wasn't getting a Christmas bonus. She wouldn't relax until she knew the SuperRobot would still be available the following week.

Unfortunately, Jake wasn't in the toy department.

"He's not here?" Holly asked Mrs. Miracle, unable to hide her disappointment.

"He's with his father just now," the older woman told her, and then frowned. "I do hope the meeting goes smoothly. It can be difficult to read the senior Mr. Finley sometimes. But I have faith that all will end well." Her eyes twinkled as she spoke.

Holly hoped she'd explain, and Mrs. Miracle obliged.

"In case you didn't hear, Jake went over the department buyer's head when he ordered those extra robots," she confided, "and that's caused some difficulty with his father. J. R. Finley has a real stubborn streak."

Mrs. Miracle seemed very well informed about the relationship between Jake and his father. "The robots are selling, though. Isn't that right?" she asked, again torn between pleasure at Jake's success and worry about laying her hands on one of the toys. The display appeared to be much smaller than last week.

"Thankfully, yes," Mrs. Miracle told her. "Jake took quite a risk, you know?"

Holly shook her head.

"Jake tried to talk Mike Scott into ordering more of the robots, but Mike refused to listen, so Jake did what he felt was best." Her expression sobered. "His father was not pleased, to put it mildly."

"But you said they're selling."

"Oh, yes. We sold another twenty-five over the weekend and double that on Monday." She nodded sagely. "I can only assume J.R. is feeling somewhat reassured."

"That's great." Holly meant it, but a shiver of dread went through her.

"Several of our competitors have already sold out," Mrs. Miracle said with a gleeful smile.

"That's terrific news." And it was — for Finley's. Parents searching for the toy would now flock to one of the few department stores in town with enough inventory to meet demand.

"How's Gabe?" Mrs. Miracle asked, changing the subject.

"He's doing fine." Holly chewed her lip, her thoughts still on the robot. "Seeing how well the robot's selling, would it be possible for me to set one aside on a layaway plan?"

The older woman's smile faded. "Oh, dear, the store doesn't have a layaway option. They haven't in years. Is that going to be a problem for you?"

Holly wasn't surprised that layaway was

no longer offered, but she figured it was worth asking. Holly clutched her purse. "I . . . I don't know." Her mind spinning, she looked hopefully at the older woman. "Do you think you could hold one of the robots for me?" She hated to make that kind of request, but with her credit card temporarily out of commission and no layaway plan, she didn't have any other choice. The payment she'd made on her card would've been processed by now, but she didn't dare risk a purchase as big as this.

"Oh, dear, I'm really not sure."

"Could you ask Jake for me?" Holly inquired. She'd do it herself if he was there.

"Of course. I just don't think I could go against store policy, being seasonal staff and all."

"I wouldn't want you to do that, Mrs. Miracle."

"However, I'm positive Jake would be happy to help if he can." She leaned closer and lowered her voice. "He's rather sweet on you."

Sweet? That was a nice, old-fashioned word. "He's been wonderful to me and Gabe."

"So I understand. Didn't he bring you dinner last night?"

Holly wondered how Mrs. Miracle knew

about that, unless Jake had mentioned it. No reason not to, she supposed. "Yes, and it was a lovely evening," she said. The only disappointment had come when Gabe asked him to help decorate the tree and Jake refused. The mere suggestion had distressed him. She hadn't realized that the trauma of those family deaths was as intense and painful as if the accident had just happened. If it was this traumatic for Jake, Holly could only imagine what it was like for his father.

"Did you know Jake and his father leave New York every Christmas Eve?" Mrs. Miracle whispered.

It was as if the older woman had been reading her mind. "I beg your pardon?"

"Jake and his father leave New York every Christmas Eve," she repeated.

Holly hadn't known this and wasn't sure what to say.

"Isn't that a shame?"

Holly shrugged. "Everyone deals with grief differently," she murmured. Her brother handled the loss of his wife with composure and resolve. That was his personality. Practical. Responsible. As he'd said himself, he couldn't fall apart; he had a boy to raise.

Sally had been sick for a long while, giving Mickey time to prepare for the inevitable — at least to the extent anyone can. He'd loved Sally and missed her terribly, especially in the beginning. Yet he'd gone on with his life, determined to be a good father.

Perhaps the difference was that for the Finleys, the deaths had come suddenly, without warning. The family had awakened the morning of Christmas Eve, excited about the holiday. There'd been no indication that by the end of the day tragedy would befall them. The shock, the grief, the complete unexpectedness of the accident, had remained an unhealed wound all these years.

"He needs you," Mrs. Miracle said.

"Me?" Holly responded with a short laugh. "We barely know each other."

"Really?"

"We met last week, remember?"

"Last week," she echoed, with that same twinkle in her eye. "But you like him, don't you?"

"Yes, I guess I do," Holly admitted.

"You should invite him for a home-cooked dinner."

Funny, Holly had been thinking exactly that. She'd wait, not wanting to appear too eager — although heaven knew that was how she felt. And of course there was the problem of her finances. . . .

"I'd like to have Jake over," she began. "He —"

"Did I hear someone mention my name?" Jake said from behind her.

"Jake!" She turned to face him as his assistant moved away to help a young couple who'd approached the department. From the corner of her eye, Holly saw that the husband and wife Mrs. Miracle had greeted were pointing at the SuperRobot. Mrs. Miracle picked up a box and walked over to the cash register to ring up the sale.

"Holly?" Jake asked.

"I need to put Intellytron on layaway but Mrs. Miracle told me you don't do that," she said in a rush.

"Sorry, no. I thought you were going to use your Christmas bonus to purchase the robot this week."

"I'm not getting one," she blurted out. She was close to tears, which embarrassed her.

"Listen, I'll buy the robot for Gabe and —"

"No," she broke in. "We already talked about that, remember? I won't let you."

"Why not?"

"Because . . . I just won't. Let's leave it at that."

He frowned but reluctantly agreed. "Okay, if that's the way you want it."

"That's the way it has to be."

"At least let me hold one for you," Jake said before she could compose herself enough to ask.

"You can do that?"

Jake nodded. "Sure. I'll set one aside right away and put your name on it. I'll tell everyone on staff that it isn't to be sold. How does that sound?"

She closed her eyes as relief washed over her. "Thank you. That would be perfect."

"Are you all right now?" He placed his hand on her shoulder in a comforting gesture.

"I'm fine. I apologize if I seem unreasonable."

"I understand."

"You do?" Holly wasn't convinced she could explain it herself. She just knew she had to do this. For Gabe, for Mickey . . . and for herself. The robot had become more than a toy. It was a symbol of her commitment to her nephew and her desire to give him the Christmas he deserved.

She saw that the department was busy and she was keeping Jake from his customers. "I have to get back to the office," she said.

He grinned. "Next time maybe you could

stay longer."

Holly smiled back. "Next time I will."

"I'll call you. You're in the phone directory?"

She nodded, hoping she'd hear from him soon. "See you, Jake."

"See you, Holly."

As she walked toward the elevator, Mrs. Miracle joined her. "Mr. Finley suggested I take my lunch hour now," she said as they stepped into the empty car together. "What I feel like having is fried chicken."

"Fried chicken," Holly echoed. "My mother, who was born and raised in the South, has a special family recipe but she hasn't made it in years. I can't even remember the last time we ate fried chicken." In this age of heart-healthy diets, her mother had focused on lean, low-carb meals.

"A special recipe?" Mrs. Miracle murmured. "I'll bet it was good."

"The best." Now that she thought about it, Holly figured she might have a copy in her kitchen. "Mom put together a book of family recipes for me when I left home. I wonder if she included that one." Fried chicken was the ultimate comfort food and would make a wonderful dinner when she invited Jake over — sometime in the new year.

"She probably did. That sounds just like her."

"You know my mother?" Holly asked, surprised.

"No . . . no, but having met you, I know she must be a very considerate woman, someone who cares about family and traditions."

What a lovely compliment. The kind words helped take the sting out of her employer's refusal to give Holly a Christmas bonus. Lindy Lee was a modern-day Scrooge as far as Holly was concerned.

That evening, as dinner heated in the microwave, Holly searched through her kitchen drawers for the notebook where her mother had written various recipes passed down through her family.

"What would you think of homemade fried chicken for Christmas?" Holly asked Gabe. It wasn't the traditional dinner but roast turkey with all the fixings was out of her budget now. If Gabe considered her fried chicken a success, she'd serve it again when Jake came over.

"I've had take-out chicken. Is that the same?"

"The same?" she repeated incredulously. "Not even close!"

"Then I've never had it." He shrugged.

"If it's not frozen or out of a can Dad doesn't know how to make it," Gabe said. "Except for macaroni and cheese in the box." He sat down at the computer and logged on to the internet, preparing to send an email to his father, as he did every night. He hadn't typed more than a few words when he turned and looked at Holly. "What's for dinner tonight?"

"Leftover Chinese. You okay with that?"

"Sure." Gabe returned to the computer screen.

Ten minutes later, he asked, "Can you invite Jake for Christmas dinner?"

"He won't be able to come."

"Why not?"

"He's going away for Christmas."

Gabe was off the internet and playing one of his games, jerking the game stick left and right as he battled aliens. "Why?"

"You'll have to ask him."

"I will." Apparently he'd won the battle because he let go of the stick and faced her. "You're going to see him again, right? You want to, don't you?"

Even an eight-year-old boy could easily see through her.

"I hope so."

"Me, too," Gabe said, then added, "Billy wants me to come over after school on

136

Friday. I can go, can't I?" He regarded her hopefully.

The boys had obviously remained friends. "I'll clear it with his dad first." Holly had been meaning to talk to Bill before this. She'd make a point of doing it soon, although she wasn't looking forward to contacting him.

The good news was that she'd found the recipe in her mother's book.

FRIED CHICKEN
(FROM *DEBBIE MACOMBER'S CEDAR COVE COOKBOOK*)

The key to crisp fried chicken is cooking at a high temperature. Stick a candy or deep-frying thermometer in the chicken as you fry to make sure the oil temperature remains between 250° and 300°F.

1 whole chicken (about 3 1/2 pounds), cut into 10 pieces
1 quart buttermilk
2 tablespoons Tabasco or other hot sauce
2 cups all-purpose flour
Salt and pepper, to taste
2 large eggs
1 teaspoon baking powder
1/2 teaspoon baking soda
Vegetable oil or shortening

1. Rinse chicken. In a large bowl or reseal-

able plastic bag, combine buttermilk and Tabasco. Add chicken pieces, turn to coat. Refrigerate, covered, for at least 8 hours and up to 16, turning the pieces occasionally. Remove chicken from buttermilk; shake off excess. Arrange in a single layer on large wire rack set over rimmed baking sheet. Refrigerate, uncovered, for 2 hours.

2. Measure flour into large shallow dish; whisk in some salt and pepper. In a medium bowl, beat eggs, baking powder and baking soda. Working in batches of 3, drop chicken pieces in flour and shake dish to coat. Shake excess flour from each piece. Using tongs, dip chicken pieces into egg mixture, turning to coat well and allowing excess to drip off. Return chicken pieces to flour; coat again, shake off excess and set on wire rack.

3. Preheat oven to 200°F. Set oven rack to middle position. Set another wire rack over a rimmed baking sheet, and place in oven. Line a large plate with paper towels. Pour oil about 1/2 inch up the side of a large, heavy skillet. Place skillet over high heat; let pan warm until oil shimmers.

4. Place half of chicken, skin-side down, in hot oil. Reduce heat to medium and fry 8 minutes, until deep golden brown. Turn chicken pieces; cook an additional eight

minutes, turning to fry evenly on all sides. Using tongs, transfer chicken to paper towel–lined plate. After draining, transfer chicken to wire rack in oven. Fry remaining chicken, transferring pieces to paper towel–lined plate to drain, then to wire rack in oven to keep warm.

Serves 4 to 6.

TEN

May you live all the days of your life.
— Mrs. Miracle

Emily Merkle smiled to herself. This latest assignment was going well. She enjoyed the ones that took place during the Christmas season most of all. She hadn't expected the romance between Jake and Holly to develop quite this quickly, so that was a bonus. Those two were very good together — and good for each other.

She attached her name badge to her sweater and hung her purse in the employee locker, then headed up to the toy department. She'd grown fond of Jake Finley. He was a kindhearted young man, a bit reserved, to be sure, but willing to take a risk he believed in. The robots were one example of that, his pursuit of Holly another.

Walking toward the elevator, she saw J. R. Finley, who'd just come into the hallway.

141

He stopped, and his eyes automatically went to her badge.

"Mrs. Miracle," he said thoughtfully. He seemed to be mulling over where he'd heard it before.

"Mr. Finley," she said in the same thoughtful tone.

"To the best of my recollection, we don't have an employee here at Finley's named Miracle."

Emily was about to identify herself, but before she could, J.R. continued.

"I pride myself on knowing the name of every employee at the Thirty-fourth Street Finley's. Including seasonal staff." He narrowed his eyes. "Just a minute. I remember my son mentioning you earlier."

"The name is Merkle," Emily told him. "Emily Merkle."

Finley shook his head. "Can't say I'm familiar with that name, either."

"If you check with HR, I'm sure —"

"You're working with my son in the toy department, aren't you?" he said abruptly.

Emily frowned. "Are you always this rude, or are you making an exception in my case?"

He blinked twice.

He was used to everyone kowtowing to him. Well, *she* wouldn't do it.

"I beg your pardon?"

Emily met his look boldly. "I was saying something, young man."

J.R.'s head reared back and he released a howl of laughter. "*Young* man? My dear woman, it's been a long time since anyone referred to me as young."

Compared to her, he was practically in diapers. "That's beside the point."

He seemed confused.

"As I was saying," Emily continued politely, "if you care to check with HR, you'll find that I was hired last week as seasonal help."

"Only last week?" J.R. smiled at her. "That explains it, then."

"It does, indeed." She started down the hallway and was surprised when J.R. kept pace with her.

"You *are* working with my son, correct?"

"Yes. The toy department is extremely busy this time of year, as you well know." She glanced pointedly at her watch, wanting him to realize she should be on the floor that very moment.

"My son made a huge error in judgment by ordering five hundred of those expensive robots."

She was puzzled by his willingness to discuss business — and family — matters with a short-term employee. But she couldn't let his comment go unchallenged. "You think so, do you?" she asked mildly.

He gave her a startled look, as if no one had dared question his opinion before. "I know so," he insisted.

Emily was curious as to why he felt Jake was wrong and he was right. "Please tell me why you're so convinced your son's about to fail."

"Good grief, woman —"

"Call me Mrs. Miracle."

"Fine, Mrs. Miracle. Do you realize exactly how many of these . . . Intellytromps he needs to sell by Christmas? That's less than two weeks from now. It'll never happen."

"They're Intelly*trons*."

"Tromps, trons, whatever. They won't sell. Mark my words. It would take a miracle." He grinned broadly, obviously thinking himself very clever.

"You called?" she said, and laughed.

J.R. apparently didn't like the fact that she'd responded to his joke with one of her own. Instead of laughing, he scowled.

"Never mind," she said with a sigh. "I just wish you had more faith in your son."

He quickly took offense. "My son is my concern."

"He *is* your concern," she agreed. "And

your future. So, it's time you trusted his judgment."

She'd really ruffled his feathers now. He grew red in the face and puffed up like an angry rooster, his chest expanding. "Now listen here. I won't have an employee talking to me as if I'm some messenger boy."

Emily stood her ground. "Someone needs to tell you the truth and it might as well be me."

"Is that so?"

He sounded like a third-grader exchanging insults on the playground.

"You need to give your son a bit of leeway to make his own mistakes instead of second-guessing all his decisions."

He opened and closed his mouth as if he couldn't speak fast enough to say what was on his mind. He thrust out one hand. "Your badge."

So he intended to fire her. "You don't want to do that," she told him calmly.

"I will not have an insubordinate employee working in my store!"

"I'm temporary help," she reminded him. "I'll be gone soon enough."

"I expect you gone *today.*"

"Sorry, I'm afraid that would be impossible. You'll need to reconsider."

Once again he couldn't seem to speak.

"Are . . . are you refusing to leave the premises?" he finally managed to sputter.

"Jacob Robert, settle down. You've always had a problem with your temper, haven't you? Now, take a deep breath and listen to me. You do not want to fire me this close to Christmas."

"Are you threatening me?" he growled. "And how do you know my middle name?"

"Not in the least," she said, answering his first question and ignoring his second.

"I'm calling Security and having you escorted from the building. Your check will be mailed to you."

"Security?" The image of two beefy security guards lifting her by the arms and marching her outside was so comical it made Emily laugh.

That seemed to infuriate him even more. "Do you find this humorous?"

"Frankly, yes." She wouldn't lie; the man was insufferable. Oh, heavens, she did have her work cut out for her. "Now, if you'll excuse me, your son needs my help."

His jaw sagged as she scurried past him and walked quickly to the elevator.

As she suspected, the toy department was in chaos. Poor Jake was run ragged — thanks, in part, to his father, who'd taken too much pleasure in making her late for her shift. That man was about to meet his match. Emily Merkle was not going to let one overstuffed, pigheaded man stand in the way of her mission.

She'd been on the floor for thirty minutes or so when J.R. unexpectedly showed up. When he saw how busy the department was, he did a double take.

"Don't stand there gawking," Emily said as she marched past him, leading a customer to the cash register. Brenda and Karen, also on duty, were bustling around, answering questions, ringing up sales, demonstrating toys.

He stared at her blankly.

"Help," she told him. "We could use an extra pair of hands, in case you hadn't noticed."

"Ah . . ." He froze, as if he didn't know where to start.

"That couple over there," Emily said, pointing in the direction of the board games. "They have a three-year-old and a six-year-old and they're looking for suggestions. Give them a few."

"Ah . . ."

"Don't just stand there with your mouth hanging open," she ordered. "Get to work!"

To his credit, J.R. rolled up his sleeves and dug in. J. R. Finley might know the name of every employee in his store — with minor exceptions, of course — but he was in way over his head when it came to recommending board games. To *her* credit, Emily kept her mouth shut.

At four o'clock there was a slight lull. "Dad," Jake greeted his father. "What brings you down here?"

J.R. squinted at Emily but didn't answer.

"Whatever it was, I'm grateful." He turned to Emily. "How many Intellytrons did we sell this afternoon?"

"Sixteen."

"Fabulous!" Jake couldn't conceal his excitement.

His father, however, looked as though he needed to sit down, put up his feet and have a cup of hot tea. In Emily's view, it would do the man good to work the floor once in a while. He might actually learn something that way.

"I came to talk to you about this woman." J.R. stabbed a menacing finger at Emily.

"Ah, you mean Mrs. Miracle," Jake said fondly. "She's a wonder, isn't she?"

"She's a nuisance," J.R. snapped. "I want her fired."

Jake laughed, which was clearly the opposite reaction of what his father expected.

"This is not a joke."

"Yes, it is," Jake insisted. "Didn't you see what a madhouse this place was? It's like that every day now. I can't afford to lose Mrs. Miracle."

Emily sauntered over to J.R.'s side and whispered saucily, "Told you so."

He shook his finger. "I don't care if I have to work this department on my own," he yelled, "I will not tolerate insubordination."

"Excuse me, Dad, I've got another customer."

"I do, too," Emily said. "But you can keep standing there for a while. You make a nice fixture."

A kid of about five stepped in front of J.R. and stared up at him. "Is that a trick, mister?"

J.R. lowered his arms. "What, son?"

The boy was completely enthralled. "The way you get your cheeks to puff out like that."

Difficult though it was, Emily managed not to laugh. The boy was quite observant. J.R. had the puffing of cheeks down to an art form.

Jake finished with his customer and hurried back to his father. "Dad, I am *not* firing Mrs. Miracle."

"No, you're not. I am," J.R. said. "It will give me great pleasure to make sure she never works in this store again."

"What did she do that was so terrible?" Jake demanded.

"She insulted me and meddled in my personal affairs," his father burst out.

"How?" Jake asked, calm and collected. He was the perfect contrast to his father, who waved both arms wildly and spoke loudly enough to attract attention from every corner of the third floor.

When J.R. didn't answer, Jake shrugged and said, "Sorry, Dad, I need her."

Emily smiled ever so sweetly.

"She's out of here," J.R. roared, making a chopping motion with his arm. She thought he resembled an umpire signaling a strike-out.

Jake shook his head. "She's our best sales associate by a mile, so if she goes, we might as well close down the entire department. You wouldn't want that, would you, Dad?"

J.R. hesitated.

"And if we close the department, you won't have a chance to prove how wrong I was by ordering five hundred Intellytrons," he said, as if that should be sufficient inducement to keep her on staff.

Emily suspected J.R. wanted Jake to fall flat on his face over this robot. He'd pay a high price for being right — and, as a matter of fact, he was dead wrong. She'd seen for herself how popular the toy was. She'd hoped it would be and had done her best to sell it. However, after the past twenty-four hours, she didn't need to try very hard; the toy sold itself. Apparently, its sudden popularity had begun like so many trends, on the West Coast. Now, the moment someone heard that Finley's still had robots in stock, they dashed over. Then they couldn't whip out their credit cards fast enough.

"I'd better stay," Emily murmured to Jake. "As much as I'd like to walk away right now, I wouldn't give your father the satisfaction."

J.R. stomped his foot.

"Are you having a temper tantrum?" she asked sweetly.

Jake only laughed. "Dad, I think it might be best if you went back to your office now. Or you could go home."

"This is *my* store and I'll stay anywhere I darn well please."

Jake leaned closer to his father and whispered, "You're scaring off my customers."

"Oh, sorry."

"We want customers, don't we, Dad? Isn't that the whole idea?"

"Don't get smart with me," J.R. muttered.

"Yes, Dad." Jake winked at Emily, who winked back.

J.R. must have caught sight of what they were doing. "What's that about?"

"What?" Emily asked, again the picture of politeness.

"What?" Jake echoed.

Seeing that he'd forfeited even the pretense of control, J.R. sighed. "Forget it."

"I can stay on, then?" Emily asked the store owner.

"Why ask me? I seem to have lost complete control of this company to a man I no longer recognize — my son." With that he marched toward the elevator that would deliver him to his private office on the fourteenth floor.

ELEVEN

People are funny. They want the front of
the bus, the middle of the road and the
back of the church.
                                    — Mrs. Miracle

Holly knew she couldn't postpone calling
Bill Carter, since the boys wanted to get
together two days from now. It would be
petty to allow her awkward relationship with
Bill to stand in the way of her nephew being friends with his son.

The problem was how to approach him.
She waited until Gabe was in bed on
Wednesday night. Then she drew in a deep
breath and looked up Bill's home number,
which she'd made a point of erasing from
her mind — and her phone. She hated feeling nervous about this. It was a courtesy
call and nothing more.

Bill picked up on the fourth ring, when
she was about to hang up, almost relieved

he hadn't answered. Then all of a sudden, she heard, "Hello."

"Bill, it's Holly."

"Do you realize what time it is?"

"Uh, yes . . . It's nine-thirty. Am I calling too late?"

He didn't respond immediately. "I know why you're calling and I —"

"You do?" So all this angst had been for nothing. She should've noticed earlier how silly she was being, how badly she'd over-reacted.

"It's about Tiffany, isn't it?"

"No . . . who's Tiffany?"

"You mean you *don't* know?"

Obviously she didn't. "Sorry, I think we're talking at cross-purposes here. I don't know any Tiffany — well, other than the one I met through work. I'm calling about Billy."

"My son?"

He sounded both relieved and worried, which confused Holly. "Listen, can we start over?" she asked.

"It's too late for that."

Just how obtuse *was* the man? "I don't mean our relationship, Bill. I was referring to our conversation."

"Just tell me why you called," he said, with more than a hint of impatience.

"I'm trying to, but you keep interrupting

me. This isn't an easy phone call for me and your attitude's not helping." If Bill was a decent human being, he should understand this was difficult and appreciate the courage it had taken her to contact him. The fact that he didn't angered her. "No wonder the two of us aren't dating anymore," she muttered.

"Okay, fine. But what's that got to do with my son?"

She sighed loudly. "Since you haven't worked it out for yourself, I'll tell you. Billy and Gabe have become friends."

"Yeah? So what?"

"Well, I —" Before she could answer his rudely phrased question, he broke in.

"Wait a minute," he said suspiciously. "How do you know my son's friends with this kid?"

The way he said it practically implied that Holly had been stalking his son. "That's the most ridiculous question I've ever heard! I know because Gabe's my nephew."

"So?"

"So Billy wants Gabe to come home with him after school on Friday."

"Fine. And this concerns you how?"

"I thought I should tell you we're related."

"That still doesn't explain why you're calling. Shouldn't Gabe's parents clear this with me? Not you."

Holly gritted her teeth at his offensive tone. What she'd ever seen in this man was completely lost on her now. At the moment, she was grateful he'd broken it off.

"I have custody of Gabe," she said calmly. She didn't feel like describing how that had come about; it was none of his business — and besides, she wanted to keep the conversation as short as possible.

"*You* have custody?"

The question grated on her nerves. "Yes, *me,* and it's working out very nicely, I might add."

"Ah . . ." Bill apparently hadn't figured out yet how to react.

Holly had no intention of allowing him to make any more derogatory comments about her mothering skills. She launched right into her question, not giving him a chance to say much of anything. "Is it still okay if Gabe comes to your house after school?"

"Uh, sure."

"Do you have the same housekeeper looking after Billy as before?"

The suspicious voice was back. "Why do you ask?"

"Because I don't want Gabe visiting Billy if there isn't any adult supervision." The after-school program only went until five-thirty, and Bill was often home much later than that, which meant the part-time house-keeper picked the boy up and then stayed at the apartment to supervise him.

"Oh, yeah, Mrs. Henry still looks after Billy from five-thirty to seven, except for the nights I have social engagements. Then she stays until I get home."

He seemed to delight in letting her know — in what he probably thought was a subtle fashion — that he'd started dating again. Well, she had social engagements, too, even if they mostly involved going out with friends, but was mature enough not to mention it. Let him think what he liked.

Holly waited a moment, hoping he'd realize how juvenile his reaction had been. "Talking civilly isn't so hard, is it?" she asked.

"No," he agreed.

"Great. Now that's settled, what time would you like me to pick Gabe up?"

"You'll pick him up?"

"Would you rather bring him back to my apartment?" That certainly made it easier for her. Maybe he didn't want Holly showing up at his house, but if so, she didn't care enough to be offended.

"I can do that," he said.

"Fine."

"Fine," he echoed.

"What time should I expect you?"

"Seven-thirty, I guess."

"I'll be here."

She was about to disconnect when Bill's soft chuckle caught her off guard. "So Gabe's your nephew, huh?"

"I already told you that."

"You did. His last name's Larson?"

"Yes, Gabe Larson." She didn't see the humor in this. "I apologize for calling so late, but I thought it would be best if you and I talked when Gabe was in bed."

"Did you think I'd refuse to let the two boys be friends?"

"I wasn't sure. Our last conversation wasn't very pleasant and, well, it seemed better to ask."

"I'm glad you did."

She was glad to hear that because he sure hadn't acted like it.

Holly met Jake for lunch on Thursday. He'd called her at the office that morning and suggested a nearby restaurant; thankfully he'd insisted on buying. She might've sounded a bit too eager to accept, because she was sick of making do with leftovers. By cutting back, packing lunches and not spending a penny more than necessary

Holly had managed to save seventy-five dollars toward the robot. According to her calculations, she'd have the funds to make the purchase but it would be close. Every cent counted.

Jake had arrived at the restaurant before her and secured a booth. "Hi," he said with a smile when she slid in across from him.

"Hi. This is nice. Thanks so much." She reached for the menu and quickly scanned the day's specials. She was so hungry, Jake would be fortunate if she could limit her selection to one entrée. As it was, she ordered a cup of wild-mushroom soup, half a turkey sandwich with salad and a slice of apple pie à la mode for dessert.

Jake didn't seem to mind.

"That was delicious," she said as she sat back half an hour later and pressed her hands over her stomach. "I probably ate twice as much as any other woman you've ever gone out with."

"It's a relief to be with someone who isn't constantly worried about her weight."

"I do watch my calories but I've been doing without breakfast, and lunches have been pretty skimpy and —"

"No breakfast?"

"That's not entirely accurate. I have breakfast, sort of. Just not much."

"And the reason is?"

Holly wished she'd kept her mouth shut. She pretended not to hear his question and glanced at her watch instead. "Oh, it's almost one. I should get back to work."

"Holly." Jake wasn't easily distracted. "Answer the question."

Her shoulders sagged. "I really do need to go."

"You're going without breakfast to save money for the robot, aren't you?"

"Sorry, I have to run." She slid out of the booth and grabbed her coat and purse. "Oh, before I forget. Gabe wanted me to invite you to come and watch us decorate our Christmas tree tomorrow night, if you can. He'll be at a friend's place and won't get home until seven-thirty."

He hesitated, and Holly knew why. "I won't be able to leave the store until at least nine," he said.

"I let Gabe stay up until ten on Friday and Saturday nights."

He hesitated again. Holly hadn't forgotten his reaction when Gabe had first mentioned decorating for Christmas. She knew that, like his father, he ignored the holiday — apart from being surrounded by all that bright and shiny yuletide evidence at the store. Perhaps it was selfish of her, but she

160

wanted to show him the joy of Christmas, prove that not all his Christmas memories were bad. She was convinced there must be happy remembrances, too, and she hoped to revive those so he could let go of the past. Holly held her breath as she waited for his response.

Jake stared into the distance for what seemed like a long time before he said, "Okay, I'll come."

Her breath whooshed out in relief and she gave him her brightest, happiest smile. "Thank you, Jake." She finished putting on her coat, hoping he understood how much she appreciated his decision.

"Can we do this again?" he asked. "It's been crazy in the toy department. Mrs. Miracle insisted I take my lunch break early — and she said I should invite you. I need to get back to work, but I wanted to see you."

"I wanted to see you, too."

They left the restaurant together and went their separate ways. Holly's spirits were high. She'd cleared the air with Bill as much as possible, and Gabe had been excited to learn he'd be able to go to his friend's house on Friday.

When she returned to work, she found her boss on the phone, talking in her usual

161

emphatic manner. Despite the fact that Holly wouldn't be receiving a Christmas bonus, she'd tried not to let that influence her job performance.

As soon as Lindy Lee saw her, she waved one arm to get her attention.

Holly stepped into her employer's office. "You're back late from lunch," Lindy said as she slammed down the phone.

"I have an hour lunch," Holly reminded her. She rarely took that long and often ate at her desk. Taking the full time allotted her was the exception rather than the rule.

"It's one-fifteen," Lindy Lee said pointedly, tapping her index finger against her wristwatch.

"And I left the office at twelve-thirty. Technically I still have fifteen minutes." Holly could see that she might have said more than necessary and decided it would be best to stop while she was ahead. "Is there something you need me to do?" she asked.

Frowning, Lindy handed her a thick file folder. "I need you to get these sketches over to Design."

"Right away." She took the folder and hurried out of the office, catching the elevator to the sixth floor. As she entered the design department she caught sight of one of the models regularly hired by the company. Tiffani White was tall, slim and elegant and she possessed about as perfect a body as one could hope to have. She was a favorite of Lindy Lee's and no wonder. The model showed Lindy's creations to their peak potential.

Tiffani saw Holly and blinked, as if she had trouble placing her, which was odd. They'd spent a fair amount of time together, since Holly had been backstage at several runway events with her.

"Lindy Lee asked me to deliver these sketches," she said to the head of the technical department. She turned to Tiffani.

"Hi, Tiff," she said casually.

"Hi." The model smiled — a smile that didn't quite reach her eyes.

Holly smiled back, but there was something strange going on. Tiffani had always been friendly. They'd even had coffee together now and then. Once, nearly a year ago when she'd been dating Bill, they'd run into Tiffani and —

Just a minute!

Thoughts and memories collided inside Holly's head. The conversation with Bill the night before played back in her mind. He'd made an unusual comment when they'd first spoken, mentioning the name Tiffany

— or rather, Tiffani, with an *i*. The pieces were falling into place. . . .

"Tiffani," Holly said. "I talked to Bill the other night."

"You did?"

"Yes, and your name came up."

The model brought one beautifully manicured hand to her mouth. "It did? Then you know?"

"Well, not everything."

"I wanted him to tell you before now, but Bill said it wasn't really any of your business. I told him that sometimes we see each other at work and it would make things better for me if you knew."

"So the two of you are . . . dating?"

"Actually we're . . . talking about marriage."

Marriage. Bill was planning to *marry* Tiffani? This didn't make sense. The model was about the least motherly woman Holly had ever met; she'd even told Holly she didn't like children. And she'd demonstrated it, too. They'd had a shoot earlier in the year with a couple of child models and Tiffani had been difficult and cranky all day. She'd made it clear that she didn't enjoy being around kids.

Holly wondered if Bill had any idea of the other woman's feelings. Probably not, she thought uncharitably. All he saw was Tiffani's perfect body and how good she looked on his arm.

In some ways, she had to concede, Bill and Tiffani were a good match. Bill had his own graphic design business and often hosted clients. Tiffani would do well entertaining, but Holly suspected she didn't have a lot to offer as a stepmother to Billy.

Yet that'd been the excuse Bill had used when he'd broken off *their* relationship.

That was exactly what it'd been. An excuse, and a convenient one. He'd wanted Holly out of his life and he didn't care how badly he hurt her to make that happen. Granted, the relationship would've ended anyway, but in the process of hastening its demise, he'd damaged her confidence — in herself and in her maternal instincts.

Bill Carter was a jerk, no question about it. Tiffani was welcome to him.

TWELVE

Be ye fishers of men. You catch 'em and
God'll clean 'em.

— Mrs. Miracle

"Can I go see Telly the robot after school?"
Gabe asked as Holly walked him to school
Monday morning.

"Not today," she said, stepping up her
speed so she'd make it to work on time. The
last thing she needed was to show up late.
As it was, Gabe would get out of school at
eleven-thirty this morning for winter break,
and there was no after-school care today.
Thankfully her neighbor, Caroline Krantz,
had children of her own, including a son,
Jonathan, who was Gabe's age, and Gabe
enjoyed going there. Today, however, he
obviously had a different agenda.

"But it's been so *long* since I saw him and
I want —"

"I know. I'm sorry, Gabe. But Christmas

166

will be here soon," she said, cutting him off.

"Do you think Santa's going to bring me my robot?"

"We won't find out until Christmas, will we?" she said, ushering him along. At the school, she bent down and kissed his cheek. "Remember, you're going to Mrs. Krantz's house with Jonathan after school."

"Yeah," he said, kicking at the sidewalk with the toe of his boot.

"Call me at the office when you get there, okay?"

"Okay."

Holly watched him walk into the building and then half ran to the subway station.

She was jostled by the crowd and once again had to stand, clutching the pole as she rode into the city. Her weekend had been everything she'd hoped for. Jake had stopped by on Friday night, arriving later than expected. She'd assembled the small artificial tree, which she'd bought years before; she would've preferred a real one but didn't want to spend the money this year. Then she'd draped it with lights, and she and Gabe had carefully arranged the ornaments. They were almost done by the time Jake came over, and Gabe insisted that he place the angel on top of the tree. Holly wasn't sure how he'd react to that request.

At first he'd hesitated until she explained it was an honor and that it meant a lot to Gabe. Then he reluctantly set the angel on the tree.

Maybe it wasn't up to her to change — or try to change — his feelings about Christmas, but she hoped to coax him by creating new memories and by reminding him of happy ones from his own childhood.

On Friday, after school and his playdate with Billy, Gabe had been exhausted by ten o'clock. Holly tucked him in, and then she and Jake had cuddled and kissed in front of the television. She couldn't remember what TV program they'd started to watch because they were soon more focused on each other than on the TV.

Thinking about Friday night with Jake made her tingle with excitement and anticipation. Bill could have his Tiffani. Holly would rather be with Jake. Their relationship held such promise. . . .

Unfortunately, Jake was so busy at the store on Saturday that a couple of quick phone calls had to suffice. On Sunday evening he came to the apartment, bringing a take-out pizza and a bottle of lovely, smooth merlot — the best wine she'd had in ages. Jake had been full of tales about the store, and especially how well Intellytron was now selling. Rumor had it that Finley's was the only place in Manhattan that had the robot available, and customers had flooded the store, many of them going straight from Santa's throne to the toy department. No one else had guessed that Intellytron would be one of the hottest retail trends of the season.

While Holly was thrilled for Jake, she was still concerned that there wouldn't be any left once she could afford to make the purchase. Jake had again assured her she didn't need to worry; he'd put one aside for Gabe. It was safely hidden away in the back of the storeroom, with a note that said it wasn't to be sold.

Holly dashed into the office just in time. She saw Lindy Lee glance at her watch but Holly knew she had three minutes to spare. While Lindy Lee might not appreciate her new work habits, she was well within the bounds of what was required. Before Gabe's advent into her life, she'd often arrived early and stayed late. That wasn't possible now, and she was paying the price for her earlier generosity, which Lindy Lee had quickly taken for granted. Still, she enjoyed her job and believed she was a credit to her employer, even if Lindy didn't agree.

"Good morning," she said to her boss,

sounding more cheerful than she felt. Holly was determined not to allow Lindy Lee's attitude to affect her day.

At noon, Holly began to check her watch every few minutes. She kept her cell phone on her desk, ready to receive Gabe's call. He should be phoning any time now; school was out, and he'd be going home with Jonathan. At twelve-thirty Holly started to worry. Gabe should be at the Krantzes'. Why hadn't he called? She felt too anxious to eat the crackers and cheese she'd brought, too anxious to do anything productive. She'd give him until one-fifteen and then she'd call.

At one-thirteen, her cell phone chirped, and she recognized the Krantzes' number. Holly heaved a grateful sigh. "Hello," she said.

"Holly?" It was Caroline.

"Oh, hi. Did everything go as scheduled? Did Gabe and Jonathan walk home from school together?"

"Well, that's the reason I'm phoning. Gabe didn't come home with Jonathan."

A chill raced down her spine. "What do you mean?"

"He told Jonathan there was something he needed to do first, so Jonathan came home by himself. I . . . I feel really bad about this."

"Where is he?" Holly asked, struggling not to panic.

"That's just it. I don't know."

There was a huge knot in Holly's chest, and she found it difficult to breathe. How could she tell her brother that Gabe had gone missing?

Panicked thoughts surged through her mind. He'd been abducted, kidnapped, held for ransom. Or even worse, simply taken, never to be seen or heard from again.

"I'll call you if I hear anything," Caroline told her. "I'd go look myself but I can't leave the children. If he's not here in an hour, we'll reassess, call the police. In the meantime, I'll phone some of the other kids' parents."

"Yes . . . Thank you." Holly disconnected the line, her cell phone clenched in her fist.

"Holly?" Lindy Lee asked, staring at her. "What's wrong?"

Holly didn't realize she'd bolted to her feet. She felt herself swaying and wondered if she was going to faint. "My — my nephew's missing."

"Missing," Lindy Lee repeated. "What do you mean, missing?"

"He didn't show up at the sitter's house after school."

Lindy Lee looked at her watch. "It's a bit early for him to be out of school, isn't it?"

"No, not today," she said, panic making her sound curt. She was torn by indecision. Her first inclination was to contact the police immediately, not to wait another hour as Caroline had suggested. They should start a neighborhood search. Ask questions.

She wondered crazily if she should get his picture to the authorities so they could place it on milk cartons all across America.

Her cell phone chirped again and she nearly dropped it in her rush to answer.

"Yes?" she blurted out.

"Holly, it's Jake."

"I don't have time to talk now. Gabe's missing and we've got to contact the police and get a search organized and —"

"Gabe's with me," Jake interrupted.

She sank into her chair, weak with relief. "He's with you?"

"Yes. He came into the city."

"On his own?" This was unbelievable!

"Yup."

"You mean to say he walked from school to the subway station, took the train and then walked to Finley's by *himself*?" It seemed almost impossible to comprehend. She held her head in one hand and leaned back in her chair, eyes closed. She remem-

172

bered what he'd said that morning, about wanting to see the robot, but she'd had no idea he'd actually try to do it.

"Would you like to talk to him?" Jake was asking.

"Please."

"Aunt Holly?" Gabe's voice was small and meek.

"So," she said, releasing a long sigh. Although the urge to lambaste him was nearly overwhelming, she resisted. "You didn't walk home with Jonathan the way you were supposed to?"

"No."

"Can you tell me why?"

"Because . . ."

"Because *what?*"

"I wanted to see Intellytron again and you said we couldn't and I thought, well, I know you have to work and everything, but I could come by myself, so I did. I remembered to take the green line and then I walked from the subway station." Despite the fact that he was obviously in trouble, there was a hint of pride in his voice.

Gabe had traveled into the city on his own just to see his favorite toy. The possibility hadn't even occurred to her. Holly suppressed the urge to break into sobs.

"I'm coming to get you right this minute,"

she declared. "Stay with Jake and Mrs. Miracle, and I'll be there as soon as I can. Now put Jake back on the phone."

His voice, strong and clear, came through a moment later. "Holly, it's Jake."

"I'm on my way."

"He'll be fine until you get here," he said.

"Thank you, thank you so much." This time, the urge to weep nearly overcame her.

"Everything's fine. Relax."

"I'm trying." She closed her cell, then looked up to see her boss standing in front of her desk.

"I take it you've located the little scoundrel?"

Holly nodded. "He came into the city on his own. Would it be okay if I brought him to the office for the rest of the day?" Taking him back to Brooklyn would be time-consuming and Lindy Lee would no doubt dock her pay. Holly needed every penny of her next paycheck. "I promise he won't make a sound."

Lindy Lee considered the request, then slowly nodded. "I enjoyed meeting Gabe that Saturday. . . . I wouldn't mind seeing him again."

Lindy Lee wanted to see Gabe again? *This* was an interesting development, as well as an unexpected one. Her employer wasn't the motherly type — to put it mildly. Lindy Lee was all about Lindy Lee.

Grabbing her coat and purse, Holly rushed over to Finley's, calling Caroline Krantz en route. The store was crowded, and by the time she reached the third floor Holly felt as though she'd run a marathon. She saw Mrs. Miracle first, and the woman's eyes brightened the instant she noticed Holly.

"You don't have a thing to worry about, my dear. Gabe is perfectly safe with Jake."

"Aunt Holly!" Gabe raced to her side and Jake followed.

"You're in a lot of trouble, young man," she said sternly, hands on her hips.

Gabe hung his head. "I'm sorry," he whispered, his voice so low she could hardly hear it.

Customers thronged the toy department, several of them carrying the boxes that held the SuperRobot. A line had already formed at the customer service desk, and she noted that a couple of extra sales associates were out on the floor today. Everyone was busy.

"You'll have to come back to the office with me," Holly told Gabe. "I'm warning you it won't be nearly as much fun as it would've been with Jonathan and his mother."

175

"I know," he muttered. "Am I grounded?"

"We'll discuss that once we're home."

"Okay, but nothing happened. . . ."

"You mean nothing other than the fact that you nearly gave me a heart attack."

Jake murmured a quick goodbye and started to leave to help a customer but Mrs. Miracle stopped him. "I'll take care of them," she said. "Besides, I believe there was something you wanted to ask Holly?"

"There was?" He looked surprised, wrinkling his brow as if he couldn't recall any such question.

"The Christmas party," Mrs. Miracle said under her breath. "You mentioned asking Holly to go with you."

Jake's mouth sagged open. "I'd thought about it, but I didn't realize I'd said it out loud." Now, instead of looking surprised, he seemed confused. "My father and I usually just make a token appearance."

"This year is different," the older woman insisted. "You need to be there for your staff. After all, the toy department's the busiest of the whole store at Christmastime. And," she continued sagely, "I predict record sales this year. Your staff needs to know you appreciate them."

"But . . ."

"I can't go," Holly said, resolving the issue. "There's no one to watch Gabe."

"Oh, but there is, my dear," Mrs. Miracle told her.

Holly frowned. Finding someone to stay with Gabe had always been a problem. She didn't want to impose on Caroline any more than she already did, especially since her neighbor wouldn't take any payment. With Jake they'd managed to work around it, which was easy enough, since Jake had mostly come to her apartment.

"I'll be more than happy to stay with Gabe while the two of you attend the party," Mrs. Miracle said.

It was generous of her to offer, but Holly couldn't accept. She shook her head. "You should be at the party yourself, Mrs. Miracle."

"Oh, heavens, no. After a full day on my feet I'll look forward to sitting in that comfy blue chair of yours. The one your parents gave you."

Before she could question how Mrs. Miracle knew about her chair, Jake asked, "Would you like to go to the party with me?" His eyes met hers, and she found herself nodding.

"Yes," she whispered. "When is it?"

"Wednesday night, after the store closes."

"Wednesday," she repeated.

"I'll pick you up at nine-thirty. I know that's late but —"

"I'll be ready."

"I'll come over a bit earlier," Mrs. Miracle added. "The two of you will have a *lovely* evening." She spoke with the utmost confidence, as if no other outcome was possible.

Holly and Gabe left a few minutes later, and Jake walked them to the elevator. "I'll see you Wednesday," he said as he pressed the button.

"Listen, Jake, you don't need to do this. I mean, it's fairly obvious you didn't intend to ask me and —"

"I'd really like it if you'd come to the party with me," he said, and she couldn't doubt his sincerity.

"Then I will," she murmured. "I'll look forward to it."

In the elevator, Holly remembered Mrs. Miracle's comment. The woman had never been to her apartment and yet somehow she knew about the chair her parents had given her. Furthermore, she seemed to know her address, too.

Oh, well. Gabe had probably told her. He obviously felt comfortable with the older woman and for that Holly could only be grateful.

THIRTEEN

Cars are not the only thing recalled by
their maker.

— Mrs. Miracle

On Wednesday at nine-fifteen, Emily stood
at Holly's door, her large purse draped over
one arm and her knitting bag in the other
hand. Holly answered, smiling in welcome.
She absolutely sparkled. In her fancy black
dress and high heels, her hair gathered up
and held in place with a jeweled comb, she
looked stunning.

"Mrs. Miracle, I can't thank you enough."
Holly stepped aside so Emily could enter
the apartment. "Tonight wouldn't be possible if not for you."

"The pleasure's all mine," she said. She
put down her bags, then unwrapped the
knitted scarf from around her neck and
removed her heavy wool coat. Holly hung
them in the hallway closet as Emily ar-

ranged her bags by the chair, prepared to settle down for the evening. The toy department had kept her busy all day and she was eager to get off her feet.

Holly followed her into the small living room. "I feel bad that you won't be attending the party."

"Oh, no, my dear." Emily dismissed her concern. "I'm not a party girl anymore." She chuckled at her own humor. "Besides, I intend to have a good visit here with my young friend Gabe."

"He's been pretty subdued since the episode on Monday. He's promised to be on his best behavior."

"Don't you worry. We'll have a grand time together." And they would.

"Hi, Mrs. Miracle."

She was surprised to see Jake standing on the other side of the room. He'd arrived early, she thought approvingly, and he looked quite debonair in his dark suit and red tie. She'd seen an improvement in his attitude toward Christmas, mostly due to Holly and Gabe. And she had it on excellent authority that it would improve even more before the actual holiday.

"Gabe's on the computer," Holly said, pointing at the alcove between the living room and kitchen. "He's had his dinner and he can stay up until ten tonight."

Gabe twisted around and waved.

Emily waved back. "I'll make sure he's in bed by ten."

Jake held Holly's coat and the young woman slipped her arms into the sleeves. "I appreciate your volunteering to watch Gabe," he said with a smile for Emily.

"As I told Holly, I'm delighted to do it." She walked over to where Gabe sat at the small desk and put her hand on his shoulder. "Now, you two go. Have fun."

Holly kissed the top of Gabe's head. "Be good."

"I will," the boy said without taking his eyes from the screen.

Holly and Jake left, and Emily had to grin as she glanced over Gabe's shoulder at the message he was emailing his father.

From: "Gabe Larson"
  <gabelarson@msm.com>
To: "Lieutenant Mickey Larson"
  <larsonmichael@goarmy.com>
Sent: December 22
Subject: Me and Aunt Holly

Hi, Dad,
I made Aunt Holly cry. Instead of going to Jonathan's house like I was supposed

to, I went to see the robot. I was afraid the store would run out before Santa got my Intellytron. Aunt Holly came and picked me up and when we were outside she started to cry. When I asked her why she was crying she said it was because she was happy I was safe.

Are you mad at me? I wish Aunt Holly had gotten mad instead of crying. I felt awful inside and got a tummy ache. She took me back to her office and made me sit quiet all afternoon. But that was okay because I knew I didn't do the right thing. Her boss is real pretty. I don't think she's around kids much because she talked to me like I was in kindergarten or something. I think she's nice, though.

You said you had a gift coming for me for Christmas. It isn't here yet. I know I was bad, so you don't have to send it if you don't want. I'm sorry I made Aunt Holly cry.

Love,
Gabe

Emily sank down in the big comfortable chair, rested her feet on the matching ottoman and took out her knitting. She turned on the television and had just finished the first row when Gabe joined her. He didn't say anything for a long time, but Emily could see his mind working.

After a while he said, "My dad's going to be mad at me."

"It was brave of you to tell him you did something you weren't supposed to," she murmured.

Gabe looked away. "I told him he doesn't need to send me anything for Christmas. He said there was a special gift on the way but it hasn't come. He probably won't send it now."

"Don't be so sure." She pulled on the skein of yarn as she continued knitting.

"What if Santa finds out what I did?" His face crumpled in a frown. "Do you think maybe he won't bring me the robot 'cause I went to Finley's by myself and I didn't tell anyone where I was going?"

"Well, now, that remains to be seen, doesn't it?"

Gabe climbed onto the sofa and rested his head against the arm. "I didn't think Aunt Holly would be so worried when I didn't go to Jonathan's house after school. She got all weird."

"Weird?"

"Yeah. When we were still at her office, all of a sudden she put her arms around my

183

neck and hugged me really hard. Isn't that weird?"

Emily shrugged but didn't answer. "Are you ready for Christmas?" she asked instead.

Gabe nodded. "I made Aunt Holly an origami purse. A Japanese lady came to my school and showed us how to fold them. She said they were purses, but it looks more like a wallet to me, all flat and skinny." He sighed dejectedly. "I wrapped it up but you can't really see where the wrapping stops and the gift starts."

"I bet Holly will really like the purse because you made it yourself," Emily said with an encouraging smile.

"I made my dad a gift, too. But Aunt Holly and I mailed off his Christmas present a long time ago. They take days and days to get to Afghanistan so we had to go shopping before Thanksgiving and wrap up stuff for my dad. Oh, we mailed him the picture of me and Santa, too. And I made him a key ring. And I sent him nuts. My dad likes cashews. I've never seen a cashew in the shell, have you?"

"Why, yes, as a matter of fact I have," she said conversationally.

Gabe sat up. "What do they look like?"

"Well, a cashew is a rather unusual nut. My goodness, God was so creative with that one. Did you know the cashew is both a fruit *and* a nut?"

"It is?"

"The fruit part looks like a small apple and it has a big stem."

The boy's eyes were wide with curiosity.

"The stem part is the nut, the cashew," she explained.

"Wow."

"And they're delicious," she said. "Good for you, too," she couldn't resist adding.

"What are you doing for Christmas?" Gabe asked.

"I've been invited to a party, a big one with lots of celebrating. I'll be with my friends Shirley, Goodness —"

"Goodness? That's a funny name."

"Yes, you're right. Anyway, the party preparations have already begun. It won't be long now."

"Oh." Gabe looked disappointed.

"Why the sad face?"

"I was going to ask you to come here for Christmas."

Emily was touched by his invitation. "I know you'll have a wonderful Christmas with Holly," she said.

"I invited Aunt Holly's boss, too."

She had to make an effort to hide her smile. This was all working out very nicely.

Very nicely, indeed.

"Lindy didn't say she'd come for sure but she might." He paused. "She said to call her Lindy, not Ms. Lee like Aunt Holly said I should."

"Well, I hope she comes."

"Me, too. I think she's lonely."

"So do I," Emily agreed. The boy was very perceptive for his age, she thought.

"I asked her what she wants for Christmas and she said she didn't know. Can you *believe* that?"

In Emily's experience, many people walked through life completely unaware of what they wanted — or needed. "I brought along a book," she said, changing the subject. "Would you like to read it to me?" She'd put the children's book with its worn cover on the arm of her chair.

Gabe considered this. "I'm not in school now. Can you read it to me?"

"The way your dad used to when you were little?" she asked.

Gabe nodded eagerly. "I used to sit on his lap and he'd read me stories until I fell asleep." His face grew sad. "I miss my dad a lot."

"I know you do." Emily set aside her knitting. "Would you like to sit in my lap?"

"I'm too big for that," he insisted.

Emily could see that despite his words he was mulling it over. "You're not too big," she assured him.

Indecision showed on his face. Gabe wanted to snuggle with her, yet he hesitated because he was eight now and eight was too old for such things.

"What book did you bring?" he asked.

"It's a special one your grandma Larson once read to your dad and your aunt Holly."

"Really? How'd you know that?"

"Oh, I just do. It's the Christmas story."

"I like when the angels came to announce the birth of Baby Jesus to the shepherds."

She closed her eyes for a moment. "It was the most glorious night," she said. "The sky was bright and clear and —"

"And the angels sang," Gabe finished enthusiastically. "Angels have beautiful voices, don't they?"

"Yes, they do," Emily confirmed. "They make music we know nothing about here on earth . . . I'm sure," she added quickly. "Glorious, heavenly music."

"They do?" He cocked his head to one side.

"You'll hear it yourself one day, many years from now."

"What about you? When will you hear it?"

"Soon," she told him. He climbed into her

187

lap and she held him close. He really was a sweet boy and would become a fine young man like his father. He'd be a wonderful brother to his half brother and half sister, as well — but she was getting ahead of herself.

"Tell me more about the angels," Gabe implored. "Is my mom an angel now?"

"No, sweetheart. Humans don't become angels. They're completely separate beings, although both were created by God."

"How come you know so much about angels?"

"I read my Bible," she said, and he seemed to accept her explanation.

"I never knew my mom," he said somberly. "Dad has pictures of her at the house. I look at her face and she smiles at me but I don't remember her."

"But you do understand that she loved you very much, right?"

"Dad said she did, and before she died she made him promise that he'd tell me every night how much she loved me."

"I know," she whispered.

"Do you think there are lots of angels in heaven?" Gabe asked.

"Oh, yes, and there are different kinds of angels, too."

"What kinds are there?"

"Well, they have a variety of different

tasks. For instance, Gabriel came to Mary as a messenger. Other angels are warriors."

"When I get to heaven, I want to meet the warrior angels."

"And you shall."

"Do you think I was named after the angel Gabriel?" he asked.

Emily pressed her cheek against the top of his head, inhaling the clean, little-boy scent of his hair. "Now, that's something you'll need to ask your father when you see him."

"Okay, I will."

"Gabriel had one of the most important tasks ever assigned," Emily said. "He's the angel God sent to tell Mary about Baby Jesus."

He yawned. "Can people see angels?"

Emily's mouth quivered with a smile she couldn't quite suppress. "Oh, yes, but most people don't recognize them."

Gabe lifted his head. "How come?"

"Not all angels show their wings," she said.

"They don't?"

"No, some angels look like ordinary people."

"How come?"

"Well, sometimes God sends angels to earth. But if people saw their wings, they'd get all excited and they'd miss the lesson God wanted to teach them. That's why

189

angels are often disguised."

"Are they always disguised?"

"No, some are invisible. Other times they look like ordinary people."

"Do angels only come to teach people a lesson?"

"No, they come to help, too."

Gabe yawned again. "How do angels help?"

"Oh, in too many ways to count."

He thought about that for a while, his eyelids beginning to droop.

"Are you ready for me to read you the story?" Emily asked.

"Sure." He rested his head against her shoulder as she opened the book. She read for a few minutes before she noticed that Gabe had fallen asleep. And she hadn't even gotten to the good part.

FOURTEEN

When you flee temptation,
don't leave a forwarding address.
— Shirley, Goodness and Mercy,
friends of Mrs. Miracle

The Christmas party was well under way by the time Holly and Jake arrived. When they entered the gala event, the entire room seemed to go still. Holly kept her arm in Jake's, self-conscious about being the center of attention.

"Why's everyone looking at us?" she whispered.

Jake patted her hand reassuringly. "My father and I usually show up toward the end of the party, say a few words and then leave. No one expected me this early."

He'd mentioned that before. Still, she hadn't realized his arrival would cause such a stir. Jake immediately began to walk through the room, shaking hands and introducing Holly. At first she tried to keep track of the names, but soon gave up. She was deeply impressed by Jake's familiarity with the staff.

"How do you remember all their names?" she asked when she had a chance.

"I've worked with them in each department," he explained. "My father felt I needed to know the retail business from the mail room up."

"You started in the mail room?"

"I did, but don't for a minute consider the mail room unimportant. I made that mistake and quickly learned how vital it is."

"Your father is a wise man."

"He is," Jake said. "And a generous one, too. But he'd describe himself as *fair*. He's always recognized the value of hiring good people and keeping them happy. I believe it's why we've managed to hold on to the company despite several attempts to buy us out."

It went without saying that Jake intended to follow his father's tradition of treating employees with respect and compensating them generously.

Ninety minutes later Holly's head buzzed with names and faces. They sipped champagne and got supper from the buffet; the food was delicious. Numerous people commented happily on seeing Jake at the party.

His father appeared at about midnight and immediately sought out his son and Holly.

"So this is the young lady you've talked about," J. R. Finley said, slapping Jake jovially on the back.

"Dad, meet Holly Larson."

J.R. shook her hand. "I'm pleased to meet you, young lady. You've made a big impression on my son."

Holly glanced at Jake and smiled. "He's made a big impression on me."

J. R. Finley turned to his son. "When did you get here?"

"Before ten," Jake said.

His father frowned, then moved toward the microphone. As was apparently his practice, he gave a short talk, handed out dozens of awards and bonuses and promptly left.

The party wound down after J.R.'s speech. People started to leave, but almost every employee, singly and in groups, approached Jake to thank him for attending the party. Holly couldn't tell how their gratitude affected Jake, but it had a strong impact on her.

"They love you," she said when they went to collect their coats.

"They're family," Jake said simply.

She noticed that he didn't say Finley's employees were *like* family but that they *were* family. The difference was subtle but significant. J.R. had lost his wife and daughter and had turned to his friends and employees to fill the huge hole left by the loss of his loved ones. Jake had, too.

As they stepped outside, Holly was thrilled by the falling snow. "Jake, look!" She held out her hand to catch the soft flakes that floated down from the night sky. "It's just so beautiful!"

Jake wrapped his scarf more securely around his neck. "I can't believe you're so excited about a little snow."

"I love it. . . . It's so Christmassy."

He grinned and clasped her hand. "Do you want to go for a short walk?"

"I'd love to." It was cold, but even without boots or gloves or a hat, Holly felt warm, and more than that, *happy.*

"Where would you like to go?" Jake asked.

"Wherever you'd like to take me." Late though it was, she didn't want the night to end. Lindy Lee had never thrown a Christmas party for her staff. Maybe she'd talk to Lindy about planning one for next December; she could discuss the benefits — employee satisfaction and loyalty, which would lead to higher productivity. Those were the

194

terms Lindy would respond to. Not appreciation or enjoyment or fun. Having worked with Lindy as long as she had, Holly suspected her employer wasn't a happy person. And she wasn't someone who cared about the pleasure of others.

"I thought this would be a miserable Christmas," Holly confessed, leaning close to Jake as they moved down the busy sidewalk. They weren't the only couple reveling in the falling snow.

"Why?" Jake asked. "Because of your brother?"

"Well, yes. It's also the first Christmas without my parents, and then Mickey got called up for Afghanistan so there's just Gabe and me."

"What changed?"

"A number of things, actually," she said. "Meeting you, of course."

"Thank you." He bent down and touched his lips to hers in the briefest of kisses.

"My attitude," she said. "I was worried that Gabe would resent living with me. For months we didn't really bond."

"You have now, though, haven't you?"

"Oh, yes. I didn't realize how much I loved him until he went missing the other day. I . . . I don't normally panic, but I did then."

Holly was still surprised by how accommodating her employer had been during and after that crisis. First Lindy Lee had allowed Gabe to come to the office and then she'd actually chatted with him. Holly didn't know what the two of them had talked about, but her employer had seemed almost pleasant afterward.

"Remember the other night when you and Gabe decorated your Christmas tree?" Jake asked.

"Of course."

"Gabe asked me about mine."

"Right." It'd been an awkward moment. Gabe had been full of questions. He couldn't understand why some people chose not to make Christmas part of their lives. No tree. No presents. No family dinner. The closest Jake and his father got to celebrating the holidays was their yearly sojourn to the Virgin Islands.

Holly knew this was his father's way of ignoring the holiday. Jake and J.R. left on Christmas Eve and didn't return until after New Year's.

She was sure they'd depart sooner if they could. The only reason they stayed in New York as long as they did was because of the business. The holiday season made their year financially. Without the last-quarter sales, many retailers would struggle to survive. Finley's Department Store was no different.

"You told Gabe you didn't put up a tree," Holly reminded him.

"I might've misled him."

"You have a tree?" After everything he'd said, that shocked her.

"You'll see." His stride was purposeful as they continued walking. She soon figured out where they were headed.

"I can't wait," she said with a laugh.

When they reached Rockefeller Center, they stood gazing up at the huge Christmas tree, bright with thousands of lights and gleaming decorations. Jake gestured toward it. "*That's* my Christmas tree," he said.

"Gabe's going to be jealous that I got to see it again — with you."

Music swirled all around them as Jake slipped his arm about her waist. "When I was young, I found it hard to give up the kind of Christmas I'd known when my mother and sister were alive. Dad refused to have anything to do with the holidays but I still wanted the tree and the gifts."

Holly hadn't fully grasped how difficult those years must've been for him.

"Dad said if I wanted a Christmas tree, I could pick one in the store and make it my own. Better yet, I could claim the one in Rockefeller Center and that's what I did."

Instinctively she knew Jake had never shared this information with anyone else.

"Well, you've got the biggest, most beautiful Christmas tree in the city," she said, leaning her head against his shoulder.

"I do," he murmured.

"Jake," she said carefully. "Would you consider having Christmas dinner with Gabe and me?"

He didn't answer, and she wondered if she'd crossed some invisible line by issuing the invitation. Nevertheless she had to ask.

"I know that would mean not joining your father when he leaves for the Caribbean, but you could fly out the next day, couldn't you?" Holly felt she needed to press the issue. If he was ever going to agree, it would be tonight, after he'd witnessed how much it meant to Finley's employees that he'd attended their party.

"I could fly out later," he said. "But then I'd be leaving my father alone on the saddest day of his life."

"I'd like to invite him, too."

Jake's smile was somber and poignant. "He'll never come, Holly. He hates anything to do with Christmas — outside of the business, anyway."

"Maybe so, but I'd still like to ask him." She wasn't sure why she couldn't simply drop this. It took audacity to invite two wealthy men to her small apartment, when their alternative was an elaborate meal in an exotic location.

She was embarrassed now. "I apologize, Jake. I don't know what made me think you'd want to give up the sunshine and warmth of a Caribbean island for dinner with me and Gabe."

"Don't say that! I want to be with you both."

"But you don't feel you can leave your father."

"That's true, but maybe it's time I started creating traditions of my own. I'd be honored to spend Christmas Day with the two of you," he said formally.

Holly felt tears spring to her eyes. "Thank you," she whispered.

She turned to face him. He smiled as she slid her hands up his chest and around his neck. Standing on the tips of her toes with a light snow falling down on them, she pressed her mouth to his.

Jake held her tight. Holly sensed that they'd crossed a barrier in their relationship and established a real commitment to each other.

"When I come, I'll bring the robot for Gabe and hide it under the tree so it'll be a real surprise."

"I'll give you the money on Friday — Christmas Eve."

Christmas Eve.

"Okay." She knew he'd rather not take it, but there was no question — she had every intention of paying.

Jake called his car service, and a limousine met them at Rockefeller Center fifteen minutes later. When he dropped her off at the apartment Mrs. Miracle was sound asleep, still in the blue chair. Jake helped her out to the car, then had the driver take her home. Holly was touched by his thoughtfulness.

Even after Jake had left, Holly had trouble falling asleep. Her mind whirled as she relived scenes and moments of what had been one of the most memorable evenings of her life. When the alarm woke her early Thursday morning, she couldn't get up and just dozed off again. She finally roused herself, horrified to discover that she was almost half an hour behind schedule.

She managed to drag herself out of bed, gulp down a cup of coffee and get Gabe up and dressed and over to the Krantzes'.

Filled with dread, Holly rushed to work.

As she yanked off her coat, she heard her name being called. Breathless, she flew into Lindy Lee's office; as usual, Lindy looked pointedly at her watch.

Holly tried to apologize. "I'm sorry I'm late. I'll make up the twenty-five minutes, I promise."

Lindy Lee raised one eyebrow. "Make sure you do."

Holly stood waiting for the lecture that inevitably followed. To her astonishment, this time it didn't. "Thank you for understanding."

"See to it that this doesn't happen again," her employer said, dismissing Holly with a wave of her hand.

"It won't . . . I just couldn't seem to get moving this morning." Thinking she'd probably said too much already, she started to leave, then remembered her resolve to discuss a Christmas party with Lindy Lee.

Aware that Holly was lingering, Lindy Lee raised her head and frowned. "Was there something else?"

"Well, yes. Do you mind if I speak freely?"

"That depends on what you have to say." Lindy Lee held her pen poised over a sheet of paper.

"I was at the employees' party for Finley's Department Store last evening," she said, choosing her words carefully. "It was a wonderful event. The employees work together as a team and . . . and they feel such loyalty to the company. You could just tell. They feel valued, and I doubt there's anything they wouldn't do to help the company succeed."

"And your point is?" Lindy Lee said impatiently.

"My point is we all need to work as a team here, too, and it seemed to me that maybe we should have a Christmas party."

Lindy Lee leaned back in her chair and crossed her arms. "In a faltering economy, with flat sales and an uncertain future, you want me to throw a *Christmas party?*"

"It's . . . it's just an idea for next year," Holly said, and regretted making the suggestion. Still, she couldn't seem to stop. "The future is always uncertain, isn't it? And there'll always be ups and downs in the economy. But the one constant is the fact that as long as you're in business you'll have a staff, right? And you need them to be committed and —"

"I get it," Lindy Lee said dryly.

Holly waited.

And waited.

"Let me think about it," Lindy Lee finally mumbled.

She'd actually agreed to think about it.
Now, this was progress — more progress
than Holly had dared to expect.

FIFTEEN

The best vitamin for a Christian is B1.
— Mrs. Miracle

Jake Finley was in love. Logically, he knew, it was too soon to be so sure of his feelings, and yet he couldn't deny his heart. Love wasn't about logic. He'd been attracted to Holly from the moment he met her, but this was more than attraction. He felt . . . connected to Holly, absorbed in her. He thought about her constantly. Over the years he'd been in other relationships, but no woman had made him feel the way Holly did.

When he arrived at work Thursday morning, he went directly to his father's office. Dora Coffey seemed surprised to see him.

"Is my father in yet?" Jake asked her.

"Yes, he's been here for a couple of hours. You know your father — this store is his life."

"Does he have time to see me?" Jake asked next. "No meetings or conference calls?"

"He's free for a few minutes." She left her desk and announced Jake, who trailed behind her.

When Jake entered the office, his father stood. "Good morning, son. What can I do for you?" He gestured for Jake to take a seat, which he did, and settled back in his own chair.

Jake leaned forward, unsure where to start. He should've worked out what he was going to say before coming up here.

"I suppose you want to gloat." J.R. chuckled. "You were right about that robot. Hardly anyone else forecast this trend. I turned on the TV this morning and there was a story on Telly the SuperRobot. Hottest toy of the season, they said. Who would've guessed it? Not me, that's for sure."

"Not Mike Scott, either," Jake added, although he didn't fault the buyer.

"True enough. And yet Mike was the first to admit he didn't see this coming."

So Scott had mentioned it to J.R. but not to him. Still, it must've taken real humility to acknowledge that he'd been wrong.

"I'm proud of you, son," J.R. continued. "You went with your gut and you were right to do it."

Jake wondered what would've happened if Finley's had been stuck with four hundred leftover robots. Fortunately, however, he wouldn't have to find out.

"I checked inventory this morning, and we have less than twenty of the robots in stock."

Jake didn't need to point out the benefits of being the only store in the tristate area with *any* robots in stock. Having a supply — even a rapidly dwindling supply — of the season's most popular toy brought more shoppers into the store and created customer loyalty.

"They're selling fast. The entire quantity will be gone before Christmas."

"Good. Good," his father said. He grinned as he tilted back in his high leather chair. "Oh, I enjoyed meeting your lady friend last night."

"Holly enjoyed meeting you."

"She's special, isn't she?"

Jake was astonished that his father had immediately discerned his feelings for Holly. "Yes, but . . . What makes you say that?" He had to ask why it had been so obvious to his father.

J.R. didn't respond for a moment. Finally he said, "I recognized it from the way you looked at her. The way you looked at each other."

Jake nodded but didn't speak.

"I remember when I met your mother." There was a faraway expression in his eyes. "I think I fell in love with Helene as soon as I saw her. She was the daughter of one of my competitors and so beautiful I had trouble getting out a complete sentence. It's a wonder she ever agreed to that first date." He smiled at the memory.

So rarely did his father discuss his mother and sister that Jake kept quiet, afraid that any questions would distract J.R. He craved details, but knew he had to be cautious.

"I loved your mother more than life itself. I still do."

"I know," Jake said softly.

"She wasn't just beautiful," he murmured, and the same faraway look stole over him. "She had a heart unlike anyone I've ever known. Everyone came to her when they needed something, whether it was a kind word, a job, some advice. She never turned anyone away." His face, so often tense, relaxed as he sighed. "I felt that my world ended the day your mother and Kaitlyn died. Since then you've been my only reason for going on."

"Well, I hope your grandchildren will be

another good reason," Jake teased, hoping to lighten the moment.

J.R. gave a hearty laugh. "They certainly will. So . . . I was right about you and Holly."

"It's too early to say for sure," Jake hedged. Confident though he was about his own feelings, he didn't want to speak for Holly. Not yet . . .

"But you *know*."

"It looks . . . promising."

Slapping the top of his desk, J.R. laughed again. "I thought so. I'm happy for you, Jake."

"Thanks, Dad." But he doubted J.R. would be as happy when he found out what that meant, at least as far as Christmas was concerned.

"Oh, before I forget," J.R. said with exquisite timing. "Dora's ordered the plane tickets for Christmas Eve. We leave JFK at seven and land in Saint John around —"

"Dad, I'll need to change my ticket," Jake said, interrupting his father.

That brought J.R. up short. "Change your ticket? Why?"

"I'll join you on the twenty-sixth," Jake explained. "Holly invited me to spend Christmas Day with her and her nephew."

J.R.'s frown was back as he mulled over

that statement. "You're going to do it?"

"Yes. I told her I would."

J.R. stood and walked to the window, turning his back to Jake. "I don't know what to say."

"Holly invited you, too."

"You told her it was out of the question, didn't you?"

More or less. "You'd be welcome if you chose to come."

Slowly J.R. turned around. "Well," he said with a sigh, "I suppose it was unrealistic of me not to realize times are changing." He paused. "I look forward to our vacation every year."

Jake had never thought of their trip to the Caribbean as a getaway. His father always brought work with him and they spent their week discussing trends, reading reports and forecasting budgets. It was business, not relaxation.

"You call it a *vacation?*" Jake asked, amused.

"Well, yes. What would you call it?" J.R. frowned in confusion.

Jake hesitated, then decided to tell the truth, even if his father wasn't ready to hear it. "I call it an escape from reality — but not from work. A vacation is supposed to be fun, a break, a chance to do nothing or else do something completely out of the ordinary. Not sit in a hotel room and do exactly the same thing you'd be doing here."

J.R.'s frown deepened.

"Admit it, Dad," Jake said. "You don't go to the islands to lounge on the beach or snorkel or take sightseeing trips. Far from it. You escape New York because you can't bear to be here over Christmas."

J.R. shook his head.

Jake wasn't willing to let it go. "From the time Mom and Kaitlyn died, you've done everything possible to pretend there's no Christmas.

"As a businessman you need the holidays to survive financially but if it wasn't for that, you'd ban anything to do with Christmas from your life — and mine."

J.R. glared at Jake. "I believe you've said enough."

"You need to accept that Christmas had nothing to do with the accident. It happened, and it changed both our lives forever, but it was a fluke, a twist of fate. I wish with everything in me that Mom and Kaitlyn had stayed home that afternoon, but the fact is, they didn't. They went out, and because their cab collided with another one, they were killed."

"Enough!" J.R. shouted.

Jake stood. "I didn't mean to upset you, Dad."

"If that's the case, then you've failed. I *am* upset."

Jake regretted that; nevertheless, he felt this had to be said. "I'm tired of running away on Christmas Eve. You can do it if you want, but I'm through."

"Fine. Spend the day with Holly if you prefer. It's not going to bother me."

"I wish you'd reconsider and join us."

J.R. tightened his lips. "No, thanks. You might think I'm hiding my head in the sand, but the truth is, I enjoy the islands."

Jake might have believed him if J.R. had walked along the beach even once or taken any pleasure in their surroundings. Instead, he worked from early morning to late evening, burying himself in his work in a desperate effort to ignore the time of year — the anniversary of his loss.

"Yes, Dad," Jake said rather than allow their discussion to escalate into a full-scale argument.

"You'll come the next day, then?"

Jake nodded. He'd make his own flight arrangements. They always stayed at the same four-star hotel, the same suite of rooms.

"Good."

Jake left the office and hurried down to

the toy department. He was surprised to see Mrs. Miracle on the floor. According to the schedule she wasn't even supposed to be in. That was his decision; since she'd volunteered to watch Gabe, he'd given her the day off.

"I didn't expect to see you this morning," he said.

"Oh, I thought I'd come in and do a bit of shopping myself."

"I didn't realize you had grandchildren," he said. In fact, he knew next to nothing about Mrs. Miracle's personal life, including her address. He'd offered to have the driver take her home and she'd agreed, but only on the condition that he be dropped off first. For some reason, he had the impression that she lived close to the store. . . .

"So how'd the meeting with your father go?" she asked, disregarding his remark about grandchildren.

"How did you know that's where I was?" Jake asked, peering at her suspiciously.

"I didn't, but you looked so concerned, I guessed it had to do with J.R."

"It went fine," he said, unwilling to reveal the details of his conversation with an employee, even if she'd become a special friend. He didn't plan to mention it to

Holly, either. All he'd say was that he'd extended the dinner invitation to his father and J.R. had thanked her but sent his regrets.

"I'm worried about J.R.," Mrs. Miracle said, again surprising him.

"Why? He's in good health."

"Physically, yes, he's doing well for a man of his age."

"Then why are you worried?" Jake pressed.

Instead of answering, the older woman patted his back. "I'm leaving in a few minutes. Would you like me to wrap Gabe's robot before I go?"

"Ah, sure," he said.

"You *are* taking it with you when you go to Holly's for Christmas, aren't you?"

"Yes."

"Then I'll wrap it for you. I'll get some ribbon and nice paper from the gift-wrapping kiosk."

"Thank you," Jake said, still wondering what she'd meant about J.R.

The older woman disappeared, leaving Jake standing in the toy department scratching his head. He valued Mrs. Miracle as an employee and as a new friend, and yet every now and then she'd say something that totally confused him. How did she know so much about him and his father? Perhaps she'd met his parents years ago. Or . . .

Well, he couldn't waste time trying to figure it out now.

Jake was walking to the customer service counter when his cell phone rang. Holly. He answered immediately.

"Can you talk?" she asked. "I know it's probably insane at the store, but I had to tell you something."

"What is it? Everything okay?"

"It's my boss, Lindy Lee. Oh, Jake, I think I'm going to cry."

"What's wrong?" he asked, alarmed.

"Nothing. This is *good*. Lindy just called me into her office. I spoke with her this morning about a Christmas party. I saw what a great time your employees had. I thought it would help morale, so I mentioned it to Lindy Lee."

"She's going to have a party?"

"No, even better than that. I can have a real Christmas dinner now with a turkey and stuffing and all the extras like I originally planned. I . . . I'd decided to make fried chicken because I couldn't really afford anything else, and now I can prepare a traditional meal."

"You got your bonus?"

"Yes! And it's bigger than last year's, so I

214

can pay for the robot now."

"That's fabulous news!"

"It is, Jake, it really is." She took a deep breath. "If you don't mind, I'd like to call your father and invite him personally."

Jake's smile faded. "I should tell you I already talked to Dad about joining us on Christmas Day."

"I hope he will."

"Don't count on it." Jake felt bad about discouraging her. "I think he'd like to, but he can't let go of his grief. He feels he'd dishonor the memory of my mother and sister if he celebrated Christmas. For him, their deaths and Christmas are all tied together."

"Oh, Jake, that's so sad."

"Yes . . ." He didn't say what he knew was obvious — that, until now, the same thing had been true of him.

"I'm looking forward to spending the day with you," Jake said, and he meant every word. "Can you meet me for lunch this afternoon?" he asked, not sure he could wait until Christmas to see her again.

When she agreed, he smiled, a smile so wide that several customers looked at him curiously . . . and smiled back.

Sixteen

Happiest are the people who give the
most happiness to others.
— Mrs. Miracle

That same morning Lindy Lee called Holly
into her office again. Saving the document
she was working on, Holly grabbed a pad
and pen and rushed inside. Gesturing
toward the chair, Lindy invited her to sit.
This was unusual in itself; Lindy Lee never
went out of her way to make Holly comfortable. In fact, it was generally the opposite.

"I've given your suggestion some
thought," she said crisply.

"You mean about the Christmas party for
next year?"

Lindy Lee's eyes narrowed. "Of course I
mean the Christmas party. I want you to
organize one for tomorrow."

"*Tomorrow?* But —"

"No excuses. *You're* the one who asked

for this."

"I'll need a budget," Holly said desperately. It was a little late to be organizing a party. Every caterer in New York would've been booked months ago. Finding a restaurant with an opening the day before Christmas would be hopeless. What was she thinking when she'd suggested the idea to Lindy Lee? Hadn't she emphasized that she was talking about the *following* year? Not this one? Holly hardly knew where to start.

Lindy Lee glared at her. "I'm aware that you'll require a budget. Please wait until I'm finished. You can ask your questions then."

"Okay, sorry." Holly wasn't sure how she was supposed to manage this on such short notice.

Lindy explained that she'd close the office at two, that she wanted festive decorations and Christmas music, and that attendance was mandatory. "You can bring your nephew if you like," she added, after setting a more than generous budget.

"In other words, the family of staff is included?"

"Good grief, no."

"But Gabe's family."

"He's adorable. He even —" Lindy Lee stopped abruptly.

Holly was in complete agreement about Gabe's cuteness, but it wouldn't go over well if Gabe was invited and no one else's children were. "The others might get upset," Holly said, broaching the subject cautiously. "I mean, if I bring Gabe and no other children are allowed, it might look bad."

Lindy Lee sat back and crossed her arms, frowning. "If we invite family, then the place will be overrun with the little darlings," she muttered sarcastically. She sighed. "*Should* we include them?"

Holly shook her head. "There are too many practical considerations. People with kids would have to go home and pick them up and . . . Well, I think it's too much trouble, so let's not."

"Okay," Lindy said with evident relief.

"I'll get right on this."

"You might invite Gabe to the office again," Lindy Lee shocked her by saying. "Maybe in the new year."

Holly wondered if she'd misunderstood. "You want me to bring Gabe into the office?"

"A half day perhaps," her boss said, amending her original thought.

"Okay." So Gabe had succeeded in charming Lindy Lee, something Holly had once considered impossible.

Lindy Lee turned back to her computer, effectively dismissing Holly. Head whirling with the difficulty of her assignment, Holly returned to her own desk. She immediately got a list of nearby restaurants and began making calls, all of which netted quick rejections. In fact, the people she spoke with nearly laughed her off the phone. By noon she was growing desperate and worried.

"How's it going?" Lindy Lee asked as she stepped out of her office to meet someone for lunch. "Don't answer. I can tell by the look on your face."

"If only we'd scheduled the party a bit sooner . . ."

"You shouldn't have waited until the last minute to spring it on me," she said, laying the blame squarely on Holly.

That seemed unfair and a little harsh, even for Lindy Lee.

"We could have our event here in the building," Lindy Lee suggested, apparently relenting. "The sixth floor has a big open space. Check with them and see if that's available."

"I'll do it right away."

"Good," Lindy said, and turned to leave.

"I'll make this party happen," Holly promised through gritted teeth.

"I'll hold you to that," Lindy Lee tossed

219

over her shoulder on her way out the door.

As soon as she'd left, Holly called the sixth floor. As luck would have it, the only time available was the afternoon of Christmas Eve — exactly what she needed. That solved one problem, but there was still an equally large hurdle to jump. Finding a caterer.

Despite the urgency of this task, Holly kept her lunch date with Jake. These last days before Christmas made getting away for more than a few minutes difficult for him. Yet he managed with the help of his staff who, according to Jake, were determined to smooth the course of romance. Mrs. Miracle, God bless her, had spearheaded the effort.

Holly picked up a pastrami on rye at the deli and two coffees, and walked to Finley's; that was all they really had time for. Now that she'd been assured of her Christmas bonus, Holly had resumed the luxury of buying lunch. When she arrived at the store, white bag in hand, Jake was busy with a customer.

Mrs. Miracle saw her and came over to greet Holly. "My dear, what's wrong?"

Once again Holly was surprised at how readable she must be. "I'm on an impossible mission," she said.

"And what's that?" the older woman asked.

Holly explained. As soon as she'd finished, Mrs. Miracle smiled. "I believe I can help you."

"You can?" she asked excitedly.

"Yes, a friend of mine just opened a small restaurant in the Village. She's still getting herself established, but she'd certainly be capable of handling this party. What are you planning to serve? Sandwiches? Appetizers? Cookies? That sort of thing?"

"The party will be in the early afternoon, so small sandwiches and cookies would be perfect. It doesn't have to be elaborate." At this point she'd accept almost anything.

"I'll get you my friend's number."

"Yes, please, and, Mrs. Miracle, thank you so much."

"No problem, my dear. None whatsoever." The older woman beamed her a smile. "By the way, I've set up a table in the back of the storeroom for you and Jake to have your lunch."

"How thoughtful."

"You go on back and Jake'll be along any minute. Meanwhile, I'll get you that phone number."

"Thanks," she said again. "Could you tell me your friend's name?"

"It's Wendy," she said. "Now don't you worry about a thing, you hear?"

Feeling deeply relieved, Holly went to the storeroom. Sure enough, Mrs. Miracle had set up a card table, complete with a white tablecloth and a small poinsettia in the middle. Holly put down the sandwich, plus a couple of pickles and the two cups of coffee.

Jake came in a few minutes later, looking harassed. He kissed her, then took his place. "It's crazy out there," he said, slumping in his chair.

"I can tell." She noticed that the rest of the staff was diligently avoiding the storeroom, no doubt under orders from Mrs. Miracle.

He reached for his half of the massive sandwich. "I sold the last of the robots this morning."

"That's wonderful!"

"It is and it isn't," he said between bites. "I wish I'd ordered another hundred. We could've sold those, as well. Now we have to turn people away. I hate disappointing anyone."

"Is there any other store in town with inventory?"

"Nope, and believe me, I've checked. Another shipment is due in a week after

Christmas but by then it'll be too late."

Holly hated to bring up the subject of Gabe's Intellytron, but she needed Jake's reassurance that the one he'd set aside hadn't been sold in the robot-buying frenzy. "You still have Gabe's, don't you?"

Still chewing on his sandwich, Jake nodded. "Mrs. Miracle wrapped it herself. It's sitting right over there." He pointed to a counter across from her. The large, brightly decorated package rested in one corner.

"I'm so grateful you did this for me," she told him. Meeting Jake had been one of the greatest blessings of the year — in so many ways.

"Thank Mrs. Miracle, too," he said. "She wasn't even supposed to be in today, but she ended up staying to help us out."

The few minutes they'd grabbed flew by much too quickly. Jake stood, kissed her again, and they left the storeroom together. As they stepped onto the floor, Mrs. Miracle handed her a slip of paper. "The name of the restaurant is Heavenly Delights and here's the number."

"Heavenly Delights," Holly repeated. "I'll give your friend a call as soon as I'm back at my desk."

"You do that."

Holly tucked the paper in her coat pocket

and nearly danced all the way to the office. With a little help from Mrs. Miracle, she'd be able to pull off a miracle of her own — she'd organize this Christmas party, regardless of the difficulties and challenges.

Once at her desk, Holly reached for the phone and called the number Mrs. Miracle had written down for her.

"Hello." A woman answered on the third ring.

"Hello," Holly returned brightly. "Is this Wendy?"

"Yes. And you are?"

"I'm Holly Larson, and I'm phoning on behalf of Lindy Lee."

"Lindy Lee, the designer?" Wendy sounded impressed.

"Yes," Holly answered. "I know I'm probably calling at the worst time, but I felt I should contact you as soon as possible." She assumed the restaurant would be busy with the lunch crowd.

"No, no, this is fine."

"I was given your phone number by Emily Miracle."

"Who?"

"Oh, sorry. Her badge says Miracle, but that's a mistake. Rather than cause a fuss, she asked that we call her Mrs. Miracle, although that's not actually her name. I apologize, but I can't remember what it is. I'm so accustomed to calling her Mrs. Miracle." Holly hoped she wasn't rambling.

"Go on," Wendy urged without commenting on all the confusion about names.

"Long story short, she suggested I call you about catering Lindy Lee's Christmas party for her employees."

"She did?"

"Yes . . . She highly recommended you and the restaurant."

"What restaurant?"

"Heavenly Delights," Holly said. Wendy must own more than one. "The location in the Village."

"Heavenly Delights," Wendy gasped, then started to laugh. "Heavenly Delights?"

"Yes." Holly's spirits took a sharp dive; nevertheless, she forged ahead. "I'm wondering if you could work us into your schedule."

"Oh, dear."

Holly's spirits sank even further. "You can't do it?"

"I didn't say that."

Her emotions went from hopeful to disheartened and back again. "Then you could?"

"I . . . I don't know what to say." The woman seemed completely overwhelmed.

Yes, I can do it would certainly make Holly's day, but the words weren't immediately forthcoming.

"Unfortunately, the party's scheduled for tomorrow afternoon — Christmas Eve." Holly suspected that, by then, practically everyone in the restaurant business would be closing down and heading home to their families. As an incentive, she mentioned the amount she could offer. The catering would take up most of the budget, with a little left over for decorations.

"That sounds fair," Wendy said.

"Would you be able to accommodate us?" she asked hopefully. "We're talking about forty people, give or take."

"I . . ."

Holly closed her eyes, fearing the worst.

"I think I could. However, there's something you should know."

"What's that?"

"First, I can't imagine who this Mrs. Miracle is."

"As I said, that isn't her real name. But I can find out for you, if you like."

"No, it doesn't matter. What I wanted to tell you is that I don't have a restaurant."

"No restaurant?" Holly's mouth went dry.

"The thing is, I've been talking with my daughter about opening one. She's attend-

226

ing culinary school. I've been praying about it, too. However, a lot of problems stand in the way — one of which is money."

"Oh."

"When I applied for a loan, the bank officer asked me what we intended to call the restaurant. Lucie and I have gone over dozens of names and nothing felt right. Our specialty would be desserts. . . . I like the name Heavenly Delights. If you don't mind, I'll borrow it."

"I . . . That's the name Mrs. Miracle gave me."

"Well, if *she* doesn't mind, we'll definitely use it." She paused. "Maybe I know her, but right now I can't figure out who she is."

"Um, so if you don't have a restaurant yet, you can't cater the event?"

"I can't," Wendy agreed. "But perhaps Lucie and her friends from culinary school could."

"Really?" Holly asked excitedly.

"Give me your number and I'll call her to see if we can make this happen."

"Great!"

Holly fidgeted until Wendy called back five minutes later. "We'll do it," Wendy told her. "Lucie talked to several of her colleagues and they're all interested. I can promise you'll *love* their menu. Lucie's already working on it."

"Fabulous. Thank you! Oh, thank you so much." Her relief was so great that she felt like weeping.

She disconnected just as Lindy returned from lunch.

"The party's all set," Holly said happily.

"Really?" She'd impressed Lindy Lee, which was no small feat.

"Christmas Eve from two to four."

Her employer nodded. "Good job, Holly."

Holly closed her eyes and basked in the glow of Lindy Lee's approval.

SEVENTEEN

We don't change God's message.
His message changes us.
> — Mrs. Miracle

Jake glanced at his watch and felt a surge of relief. Five-thirty on Christmas Eve; in half an hour, the store would close its doors for the season.

Finley's would open again on the twenty-sixth for the year-end frenzy. He felt good that toy sales for this quarter were twenty percent higher than the previous year. He attributed the boost in revenue to Intellytron the SuperRobot. Jake felt vindicated that his hunch had been proven right. He'd be proud to take these latest figures to his father. While the robot alone didn't explain the increase, the fact that it was available at Finley's had brought new customers into the store.

Holly was occupied with her boss and the

Christmas party, which she'd arranged for Lindy Lee at the last moment. The poor girl had worked herself into a nervous state to pull off the event, and Jake was confident that the afternoon had gone well. He knew Holly had obsessed over each and every detail.

No doubt exhausted, she'd go home to her Brooklyn apartment as soon as she was finished with the cleanup. Jake would come by later that evening to spend time with her and Gabe. The three of them would enjoy a quiet dinner and then attend Christmas Eve services at her church.

It felt strangely luxurious not to be rushing away from the city with his father, although Jake was saddened that he hadn't been able to convince J.R. to join them on Christmas Day.

His cell chirped, and even before he looked, Jake knew it was Holly.

"Hi," he said. "How'd the party go?"

"Great! Wonderful. Even Lindy Lee was pleased. The caterers did a fabulous job, above and beyond my expectations. Wendy told me that Heavenly Delights plans to specialize in desserts and they should. Everything was spectacular."

"I'm glad."

"Don't forget to bring over Gabe's gift

tonight," she said in a tired voice. As he'd expected, Holly was worn out.

"Sure thing."

"We'll hide it in my bedroom until he goes to sleep, and then we can put it under the tree. That way it'll be the first thing he sees Christmas morning."

"Sounds like a plan."

"I'll distract him when you arrive so you can shove it in my closet."

"Okay."

She hesitated. "Are you sure you can't talk your father into coming for Christmas dinner?"

"I don't think so, Holly. He isn't ready to give up his . . . vacation." He nearly choked on the word.

"Ask him again, would you?" she said softly.

"I will," he agreed with some reluctance, knowing it wouldn't have any effect.

"And thank Mrs. Miracle for me. She saved the day with this recommendation."

"Of course. Although I believe she's already left."

"She'll be back, won't she?"

"As seasonal help, she'll stay on until the end of January when we finish inventory." The older woman had been a real success in the department. She'd reassured parents and entertained their kids. If she was interested, Jake would like to offer her full-time employment.

He ended his conversation with Holly and went into the storeroom to pick up Gabe's robot.

He stopped short. The package that had lain on the counter, the package so beautifully wrapped by Mrs. Miracle, was missing.

Gone.

"Karen," Jake said, walking directly past a customer to confront one of the other sales associates. If this was a practical joke, he was not amused. "Where's the robot that was on the counter in the storeroom?" he demanded, ignoring the last-minute shopper she was assisting.

Karen blinked as though he was speaking in a foreign language. "I beg your pardon?"

"The wrapped gift in the storage room?" he repeated.

"I . . . I don't have a clue."

"You know what I'm talking about, don't you?"

Her face became flushed. "I'm not sure."

"It was wrapped and ready for delivery and now it's missing." Jake couldn't believe anyone would steal the robot. He knew his employees, and there wasn't a single one who was capable of such a deed. He'd stake his career on it.

"Did you ask John?"

"No." Jake quickly sought out the youngest sales associate. John had just finished with a customer and looked expectantly at Jake.

"The robot's missing," he said without preamble.

John stared back at him. "The one in the storeroom?"

"Are there any others in this department?" he snapped. If there were, he'd grab one and be done with it. However, no one knew better than Jake that there wasn't an Intellytron to be had.

"I saw it," Gail said, joining them.

Relief washed over Jake. Someone had moved it without telling him; that was obviously what had happened. The prospect of facing Holly and telling her he didn't have the robot didn't bear thinking about.

That morning, the moment she'd received her Christmas bonus, Holly had rushed over to Finley's to pay for the toy. Her face had been alight with happiness as she described how excited Gabe would be when he found his gift under the Christmas tree. That robot meant so much to the boy. If Jake didn't bring it as promised, Holly might not forgive him. He hoped that wouldn't happen, but the thought sent a chill through him nonetheless.

Frances, another sales associate, came over, too. "Mrs. Miracle had it," she said.

"When?"

"This morning," Frances explained. "She didn't mention it to you?"

"No." Jake shook his head. "What did she do with it?"

Frances stared down at the floor. "She sold it."

"*Sold* it?" Jake exploded. This had to be some kind of joke — didn't it? "How could she do that? It was already paid for by someone else." That robot belonged to Gabe Larson. She knew that as well as anyone.

"Why would she sell it?" he burst out again, completely bewildered.

"I . . . I don't know. You'll have to ask her," Frances said. "I'm so sorry, Mr. Finley. I'm sure there's a logical explanation."

There'd better be. Not that it would help now.

Sick at heart, Jake left the department and went up to his father's office. Dora had already gone home; the whole administrative floor was deserted. He didn't know what he'd tell Holly. He should've taken the robot to his apartment and kept it there. Then he could've been guaranteed that nothing like this would happen. Still, berating himself now wouldn't serve any useful purpose.

Preparing for his flight, J. R. Finley was busy stuffing paperwork in his computer case when Jake entered the office. J.R. looked up at him. "What's the matter with you? Did you decide to come with me, after all?"

"No. Have you decided to stay in New York?" Jake countered.

"You're kidding, right?"

Jake slumped into a chair and ran his fingers through his hair. "Gabe's robot is missing," he said quietly. "Emily Miracle, or whatever her name is, sold it."

"Mrs. Miracle?" J.R.'s face tightened and he waved his index finger at Jake. "I told you that woman was up to no good, butting into other people's business. She's a troublemaker. Didn't I tell you that?"

"Dad, stop it. She's a sweet grandmotherly woman."

"She's ruined a little boy's Christmas and you call that *sweet?*" He made a scoffing sound and resumed his task of collecting papers and shoving them into his case.

"Do you have any connections — someone who can locate a spare Intellytron at the last minute?" This was Jake's only hope.

Frowning, his father checked his watch. "I'll make some phone calls, but I can't promise anything."

Jake was grateful for whatever his father could do. "What about your flight?"

J.R. looked at his watch again and shrugged. "I'll catch a later one."

Jake started to remind his father that changing flights at this point might be difficult, but stopped himself. If J.R. was going to offer his assistance, Jake would be a fool to refuse.

"I'll shut down the department and meet you back here in twenty minutes," Jake said.

His father had picked up his phone and was punching out numbers. One thing Jake could be assured of — if there was a single Intellytron left in the tristate area, J.R. would locate it and have it delivered to Gabe.

He hurried back to the toy department and saw that the last-minute customers were being ushered out, bags in hand, and the day's sales tallied. The store was officially closed. His staff was waiting to exchange Christmas greetings with Jake so they could go home to their families.

"Is there anything we can do before we

leave?" John asked, speaking for the others.

"No, thanks. You guys have been great. Merry Christmas, everyone!"

As soon as they'd left, he got Mrs. Miracle's contact information and called the phone number she'd given HR. To his shock, a recorded voice message informed him that the number was no longer in service. That wasn't the only shock, either — she'd handed in her notice that afternoon.

He groaned. Mrs. Miracle was unreachable and had absconded with precious information regarding the robot — like why she'd sold it and to whom.

Jake returned to his father's office to find him pacing the floor with the receiver pressed to his ear. J.R. glanced in Jake's direction, then quickly looked away. That tight-lipped expression told Jake everything he needed to know — his father hadn't been successful.

He waited until J.R. hung up the phone.

"No luck," Jake said, not bothering to phrase it in the form of a question.

J.R. shook his head. "Everyone I talked to said as far as they knew we're the only store in five states to have the robot."

"*Had.* We sold out."

"Apparently there isn't another one to be

found anywhere till after Christmas."

Jake had expected that. A sick feeling attacked the pit of his stomach as he sank into a chair and sighed loudly. "I appreciate your help, Dad. Thanks for trying."

"I'm sorry I couldn't do more." J.R. nodded and placed a consoling hand on Jake's shoulder. "I know how you feel."

Jake doubted that but he wasn't in the mood to argue.

"Holly's special," J.R. said. "I've known that since the first time you mentioned her."

"She is." Jake was in full agreement there.

"If it'd been your mother who needed that thing, I would've moved heaven and earth to make sure she got it."

He reconsidered. Maybe his father *did* know what he was feeling. He'd done his utmost to keep Holly and Gabe from being disappointed. Unfortunately, nothing he or J.R. did now would make any difference. It was simply too late.

"Every Intellytron in New York State and beyond is wrapped and under some youngster's tree," J.R. said.

Jake rubbed his face. "I'll come up with something to tell Holly and Gabe," he said, thinking out loud.

"Is there anything else the boy might like?" his father asked.

The only toy Gabe had referred to, at least in Jake's hearing, was the robot. He'd even risked Holly's wrath and traveled into the city on his own just to see it again and watch it in action.

"What about a train set?" his father suggested. "Every little boy wants a train set."

Jake had. He'd longed for one the Christmas his mother and sister had died. But there'd been no presents the next morning or any Christmas morning since the accident.

"He might," Jake said. "But —"

"Well, we have one of those."

Jake wondered what his father was talking about. As head of the toy department Jake was well aware of the inventory left in stock and there were no train sets. This season had been record-breaking in more ways than one; not only the robot but a number of other toys had sold out. The trains, a popular new doll, a couple of computer games . . . "Exactly where is there a train set?" he asked. "Unless you mean the one in the window . . ."

"Not the display train. A brand-new one. Except that it's twenty-one years old." J.R. swallowed visibly. "I have it," he said. "It's still wrapped in the original paper. Your mother bought it for you just before . . ."

He didn't need to finish the sentence.

"Mom bought me the train set I wanted?" Jake asked, his voice hoarse with emotion.

J.R. grinned. "You were spoiled, young man. Your mother loved you deeply. And your little sister adored you."

A sense of loss hit him hard and for a moment that was all Jake could think about. "You kept the train set all these years?" he finally asked.

J.R. nodded solemnly. "I always meant to give it to you but I could never part with it. In a way, holding on to it was like . . . having your mother still with me. I could pretend it was Christmas Eve twenty-one years ago and she hadn't died. Don't worry, I didn't *actually* believe that, but I could indulge the fantasy of what Christmas should've been. That train set made the memory so real. . . ."

"And you're willing to give it up for Gabe?"

"No" was his father's blunt reply. "I'm willing to give it up for *you.*"

Jake smiled and whispered, "Thanks, Dad."

"You're welcome. Now we've got a bit of digging to do. I don't remember where I put that train set but I know it's somewhere in the condo. Or maybe the storage locker.

Or . . ."

"Do we have time? Did you change your flight?"

"Flight?" J.R. repeated, then seemed to remember he was scheduled to fly out that evening. Shaking his head, he muttered, "It's fine. I'll catch one tomorrow if I have to."

Jake didn't want to pressure his father, but he'd promised Holly he'd invite J.R. to dinner at her apartment. Although he'd already tried once, he'd ask again. If he was going to disappoint her on one front, then the least he could do was surprise her on another.

"Since you're apparently staying over . . ." he began.

"Yes?"

"Have Christmas dinner with Holly and Gabe and me tomorrow afternoon. Will you do that, Dad?"

His father took a long moment to consider the invitation. Then, as if the words were difficult to say, he slowly whispered, "I believe I will. Something tells me your mother would want me to."

EIGHTEEN

God isn't politically correct.
He's just correct.
— Mrs. Miracle

Holly set the phone down and forced herself to keep the smile on her face. Gabe's robot was missing. Because Gabe was in earshot, she couldn't ask Jake the questions that clamored in her mind. He'd said something about Mrs. Miracle, but Holly had been too disheartened to remember what followed.

Adding to her distress, Jake had said there was something he needed to do with his father, which meant he'd have to renege on dinner that night. In addition to the bad news about the missing robot, Jake had passed on some good news, too. Evidently his father had changed his plans and would be joining them on Christmas Day, after all, which delighted Holly and greatly encouraged her. She recognized that this was no small concession on J.R.'s part.

"Isn't Jake coming for dinner?" Gabe asked, looking up from his handheld video game. He lay on the sofa as he expertly manipulated the keys.

"I . . . No. Unfortunately, Jake has something else he has to do," Holly explained, doing her best to maintain an even voice. "Something really important," she emphasized.

Gabe frowned and sat up. "What's more important than Christmas Eve?"

Again Holly made an effort to pretend nothing was wrong. "We'll have to ask when we see him tomorrow," she said airily.

Her nephew slouched back onto the sofa. His downcast look prompted Holly to sit beside him. She felt as depressed as Gabe did, but was trying hard not to show it. In the larger scheme of life, these disappointments were minor. Nevertheless, she'd hoped to give Gabe a very special gift this year. And she'd hoped — so had Gabe — to spend Christmas Eve with Jake.

"Did Jake promise to come tomorrow?"

"He'll be here."

"But he said he'd come for dinner tonight, too — and he didn't."

"We'll have a wonderful time this evening, just the two of us." She slipped her arm around his small frame and squeezed gently.

Gabe didn't seem too sure of that. "Can I email my dad?"

"Of course." Holly would come up with ways to keep them both occupied until it was time to walk to church for the Christmas Eve service. They could watch a Christmas movie; Gabe might enjoy *The Bishop's Wife,* Holly's favorite, or *A Christmas Carol* with Alastair Sim as the ultimate Scrooge. Still cheering herself up, she headed into her kitchen to start frying the chicken, which had been marinating in buttermilk since six that morning. They'd have turkey tomorrow, but tonight she'd make the meal she associated with her mother . . . with comfort.

Gabe leaped up from the sofa and hurried into the kitchen. "Can we invite Mrs. Miracle for dinner?" he asked excitedly.

"Oh, Gabe, I wish we'd thought of that sooner."

"I like Mrs. Miracle."

"I like her, too." The older woman had never mentioned whether she had family in the area, which made Holly wonder if she was spending this evening by herself.

Gabe returned to writing his email. "Dad's surprise didn't come, did it?" he said in a pensive voice.

Holly suddenly realized it hadn't. This complicated everything. Not only wouldn't she be able to give her nephew the only toy he'd requested for Christmas, but the gift his father had mailed hadn't arrived, either.

"He might be mad at me for going into the city by myself," Gabe murmured.

"Oh, sweetie, I'm positive that's not it."

Before she could finish her reassurances, the doorbell chimed. Hoping, despite everything, that it was Jake, Holly answered the door, still wearing her apron. To her astonishment, Emily Miracle was standing in the hall.

"I hope you don't mind me dropping in unexpectedly like this."

"Mrs. Miracle! Mrs. Miracle!" Gabe rushed to the door. "We were just talking about you." He grabbed her free hand and tugged her into the apartment. "Can you stay for dinner? Aunt Holly's making fried chicken and there's corn and mashed potatoes and cake, too. You can stay, can't you? Jake said he was coming and now he can't."

"Oh, dear," Emily said, laughing softly. "I suppose I could. I came by to bring you my Christmas salad. It's a family favorite and I wanted to share it with you."

"That's so nice of you, Emily," Holly said, adding a place setting to the table. Her mood instantly lightened.

"Jake *said* he'd come," Gabe pouted.

"He's doing something important," Holly reminded her nephew.

"I'm sure he is," Emily said, giving Holly a covered ceramic bowl and removing her coat. "It isn't like Jake to cancel at the last moment without a good reason. He's a very responsible young man — in his personal life and in business, too. He'll do his father proud." She held out her hands for the bowl.

"You mean *does* his father proud," Holly corrected, passing it back. She had every confidence that Jake would one day step up to the helm at Finley's, but that was sometime in the future. Jake seemed to think it might take as long as five years, and he said that suited him fine.

"Yes, that's what I mean. I've enjoyed working with him this Christmas season." Emily made her way into the kitchen and put her salad in the refrigerator.

"Can you come to church with us?" Gabe asked, following her. "It's Christmas Eve, and there's a special program and singing, too."

"I'd like that very much, but unfortunately I already have other plans."

"We're grateful you could have dinner with us," Holly said. She waited until Gabe

246

had left the room before she asked Emily about the robot.

"Do you have any idea what happened to the you-know-what Jake put aside?" She spoke guardedly because the apartment was small and she wanted to ensure that Gabe didn't hear anything that would upset him.

Mrs. Miracle was about to answer when he dashed into the kitchen again.

Grasping the situation, she immediately distracted him. "Do you want to help me fill the water glasses?" she asked.

"Okay," Gabe agreed.

Emily poured water into the pitcher, which she handed to Gabe. Holding it carefully, he walked over to the dining area, which was actually part of the living room. The older woman turned to Holly. "I think there was a misunderstanding between Jake and me," she said in a low voice. "I'll clear everything up as soon as I can."

"Please do," Holly whispered. She tried to recall her conversation with Jake. He seemed to imply that Emily had sold the robot to someone else. That didn't seem possible. She'd never do anything to hurt a little boy; Holly was convinced of it.

The fried chicken couldn't have been better; in fact, it was as good as when her mother had prepared this dish. Holly had wanted tonight's meal to be memorable for Gabe, and because Mrs. Miracle was with them, it was.

During dinner, Emily entertained them with story after story of various jobs she'd taken through the years. She'd certainly had her share of interesting experiences, working as a waitress, a nanny, a nurse and now a salesperson.

All too soon, it was time to get ready for church. Holly reluctantly stood up from the table.

"Everything was lovely," Mrs. Miracle told her with a smile of appreciation. "I've never had chicken that was more delicious." She carried her empty dessert plate to the kitchen sink. "And that coconut cake . . ."

"I liked the sauce best," Gabe chimed in, putting his plate in the sink, too.

"I loved the salad," Holly said, and was sincere. "I hope you'll give me the recipe."

"Of course. I'll be happy to write it out for you now if you'll get me some paper and a pen."

Holly tore a page from a notebook and grabbed Gabe's Santa pen; minutes later, Mrs. Miracle handed her the recipe with a flourish. "Here you go." Then she frowned at her watch. "Oh, my. I hate to run, but I'm afraid I must."

"No, no, don't worry," Holly assured her. "We have to leave for church, anyway. I'm just glad you could be with us this evening. It meant a lot to Gabe and me."

The older woman bent down and kissed the boy's cheek. "This is going to be a very special Christmas for you, young man. Just you wait. It's one you'll remember your whole life. Someday you'll tell your grandchildren about the best Christmas of your life."

"Do you really think so?" Gabe asked, eyes alight with happiness.

She reached for her coat and put it on before she hugged Holly goodbye. "It's going to be a special Christmas for you, as well, my dear."

Holly smiled politely. Maybe Mrs. Miracle was right, but it definitely hadn't started out that way.

Gabe woke at six o'clock Christmas morning. He knocked on Holly's bedroom door and shouted, "It's Christmas!" Apparently he suspected she might have forgotten.

Holly opened one eye. Still half-asleep, she sat up and stretched her arms above her head.

"Can we open our presents?" Gabe asked, leaping onto her bed.

"What about breakfast?" she said.

"I'm not hungry. You aren't, either, are you?" The question had a hopeful lilt, as though any thought of food would be equally irrelevant to her.

"I could eat," she said.

Gabe's face fell.

"I could eat . . . later," she amended.

His jubilant smile reappeared.

"Shall we see what Santa brought you?" she asked, tossing aside her covers. She threw on her housecoat and accompanied him into the living room, where the gifts beneath the small tree awaited their inspection.

Gabe fell to his knees and began rooting through the packages she'd set out the night before, after he'd gone to sleep. He must've known from the size of the wrapped boxes that the robot wasn't among them. He sat back on his heels. "Santa didn't get me Intellytron, did he?"

"I don't know, sweetie. I hear Santa sometimes makes late deliveries."

"He does?" Hope shone in his face. "When?"

"That I can't say." Rather than discuss the subject further, Holly hurried into the kitchen.

While she put on a pot of coffee, Gabe arranged the gifts in two small piles. Most of them had been mailed by Holly's parents, and Gabe's didn't take long to unwrap. He was wonderful, sweetly expressing gratitude and happiness with his few gifts. A number of times Holly had to wipe tears from her eyes.

"I hope you're not too disappointed," she said when she could speak. "I know how badly you wanted the robot — and I'm sure Santa has one for you but it might be a little late."

Gabe looked up from the new video game she'd purchased on her way home from work. "I bet I'll still get Intellytron. Mrs. Miracle said this was going to be my best Christmas ever, remember? And it wouldn't be without my robot." He jumped up and slid his arms around Holly's neck and gave her a tight hug.

She opened her gifts after that — a book from her parents, plus a calendar and a peasant-style blouse. And the origami purse from Gabe, which brought fresh tears to her eyes.

They had a leisurely breakfast of French toast and then, while Gabe played with his new video game, Holly got the turkey in the oven. The doorbell rang around eleven o'clock.

251

Jake and his father came in, carrying a large wrapped box between them. Holly's heartbeat accelerated. It must be Intellytron, although the box actually seemed too big.

"Merry Christmas," Jake said, and held her close. "Don't get excited — this isn't what you think it is," he whispered in her ear just before he kissed her.

"Merry Christmas, young man," J.R. said, and shook Gabe's hand.

"What's that?" Gabe asked, eyeing the box Jake had set on the carpet.

"Why don't you open it and see?" J.R. suggested.

Jake stood at Holly's side with his arm around her waist. "I'm sorry I had to cancel last night," he said in a low voice.

"It's fine, don't worry."

"Mrs. Miracle came over," Gabe said as he sat on the floor beside the box.

"Emily Miracle?" Jake frowned. "Did she happen to deliver something?" he asked, his eyes narrowing.

"She brought a Christmas salad for dinner," Gabe told him, tearing away the ribbon. He looked up. "We didn't eat it all. Do you want to taste it?" He wrinkled his nose. "For green stuff, it was pretty good."

"I wouldn't want to ruin my dinner," J.R.

said, smiling down at him. "Go ahead, young man, and let 'er rip."

Gabe didn't need any encouragement. He tore away the wrapping paper. "It's a train set," he said. "That was the second thing on my Christmas list, after Intellytron. Can we set it up now?"

"I don't see why not," Jake told him and got down on his knees with Gabe. "I wanted one when I was around your age, too."

"Did you get one?" Gabe asked.

Jake looked at his father, who sat on the sofa, and nodded. "I certainly did, and it was the best train set money could buy."

Gabe took the engine out of the box. "Wow, this is heavy."

"Let's lay out the track first, shall we?"

Holly sat on the sofa next to Jake's father. "I'm so glad you could have dinner with us."

"I am, too." A pained look came over him and he gave a slight shake of his head. "I was sure I'd never want to celebrate Christmas again, but I've decided it's time I released the past and started to prepare for the future."

"The future?" she repeated uncertainly.

"Grandchildren," J.R. said with a sheepish grin. "I have the distinct feeling that my son has met the woman he's going to love as much as I loved his mother."

Embarrassed, Holly looked away. With all her heart she hoped she was that woman.

"Jake would be furious with me if he knew I'd said anything. It's too soon — I realize that. He probably isn't aware of how strongly he feels, but I know. I've seen my son with other women. He's in love with you, the same way I was in love with Helene."

Holly was about to make some excuse about dinner and return to the kitchen when the doorbell chimed again. Everyone looked at her as if she knew who it would be.

"I . . . I wonder who that is," she murmured, walking to the door.

"It could be Mrs. Miracle," Gabe said hopefully.

Only it wasn't.

Holly opened the apartment door to find her brother standing there in his army fatigues, wearing a smile of pure happiness. In his arms he held a large wrapped box.

"Mickey!" she screamed. He put down the box and hugged her fiercely.

"Dad!" Gabe flew off the floor as though jet-propelled and launched himself into his father's arms.

Eyes closed, Mickey held the boy for a

long, long time.

Merry Christmas, Holly thought, tears slipping down her face. Just as Emily Miracle had predicted, this was destined to be the best Christmas of Gabe's life.

BABY ARUGULA SALAD WITH GOAT CHEESE, PECANS AND POMEGRANATE SEEDS
(FROM *DEBBIE MACOMBER'S CEDAR COVE COOKBOOK*)

This salad is a lively blend of sharp arugula, tangy goat cheese, mellow pecans and tart pomegranates. If you can't find arugula, substitute any delicate salad green.

1 small shallot, minced
3 tablespoons balsamic vinegar
1 teaspoon Dijon mustard
Salt and pepper, to taste
1/2 cup extra-virgin olive oil
10 to 12 cups baby arugula (about 10 ounces)
1 cup pomegranate seeds (from one pomegranate)
1/2 cup toasted pecans, chopped

1 cup crumbled goat cheese

1. In a measuring cup, whisk shallot, vinegar, mustard, salt and pepper until combined. Slowly pour oil in a stream until blended.
2. In a large serving bowl, combine arugula, pomegranate seeds and pecans. Add dressing; toss to coat. Top salad with cheese; toss once.

TIP: Extra-virgin olive oil, which comes from the first cold pressing of the olives, has a stronger, purer flavor than virgin olive oil. Since it is more expensive, most cooks prefer to use it only for salad and other uncooked dishes. Virgin olive oil is better for sautéing.

Serves 8.

NINETEEN

Searching for a new look?
Have your faith lifted!
— Mrs. Miracle

Mickey stepped into the apartment, still holding Gabe, and extended his hand to Jake. "You must be Jake Finley."

"And you must be Holly's brother, Mickey."

"I am."

"What's in there?" Gabe asked, looking over his father's shoulder at the large box resting on the other side of the open door.

"That's a little something Santa asked me to deliver," Mickey told his son. Gabe squirmed out of his arms and raced back into the hallway. He stared at Holly and his grin seemed to take up his whole face. "I think I know what it is," he declared before pushing the box inside. "Aunt Holly told me Santa sometimes makes deliveries late."

No one needed to encourage him to unwrap the gift this time. He tore into the wrapping paper, which flew in all directions. As soon as he saw the picture of Intellytron on the outside of the box, Gabe gave a shout of exhilaration.

"It's my robot! It's my robot!"

"Wherever did you find one?" J.R. asked Mickey. The older man stepped forward and extended his hand. "J. R. Finley," he said.

"He bought it at Finley's," Jake answered in a confused tone.

"Our department store?" J.R. sounded incredulous. "When?"

"My guess is that it was late on Christmas Eve." Again, Jake supplied the answer.

"And how do you know all this?" Holly had a few questions of her own.

"Because that's the gift wrap Mrs. Miracle used."

"But . . . who sold it to him?" J.R. appeared completely befuddled by this latest development.

"Mrs. Miracle," Jake and Holly murmured simultaneously.

"He's right," Mickey said as he sat on the couch next to his son, who remained on the floor. "I remember her name badge. Mrs. Miracle. We talked for a few minutes."

Thankfully, Gabe was too involved with

his robot to listen.

"I had a chance to go into the city yesterday," Mickey told them.

"Wait." Holly held up her hand. "You've got some splainin' to do, Lieutenant Larson. Why are you in New York in the first place?"

Mickey laughed. "Don't tell me you don't want me here?"

"No, no, of course I do! But you might've said something."

"I couldn't."

"Security reasons?" Holly asked.

"No, just that I wasn't sure I'd get the leave I was hoping for. I've been sent back for specialized training — I'll be at Fort Dix for the next six weeks. I didn't want to say anything to Gabe yet, in case it fell through. I could tell from his emails that he was starting to adjust to life here with you. It would've been cruel to raise his hopes, only to have Uncle Sam dash them. Turns out I was on duty until nine this morning . . . so here I am. I thought I'd bring Gabe his Christmas surprise."

"You might've mentioned it to *me*," Holly said with more than a little consternation.

"True, but I had to take your poor track record with keeping secrets into consideration."

"I can keep a secret," she insisted.

"Oh, yeah? What about the time you told Candi Johnson I had a crush on her?"

"I was twelve years old!"

Jake chuckled and she sent him a stern look. If Mickey had asked her not to say anything about his possible visit, she wouldn't have uttered a word. Then it occurred to her that he'd hinted at it when he referred to the surprise he was sending Gabe. Fantastic, stupendous, *exhilarating* though this was, a Christmas visit was the last thing she'd expected.

"But why buy the robot?" Holly asked. "I told you I'd get it for Gabe."

"Yes, but you were going without lunches —"

"True," she interrupted, whispering so Gabe wouldn't hear. "Then Lindy Lee had a change of heart and decided to give me a Christmas bonus, after all."

Mickey shrugged. "You didn't say anything to me. Not that it matters because *I* wanted to get this for Gabe."

"I didn't tell you I received my bonus?"

"You've done enough for the two of us," Mickey told her, his eyes warm with appreciation. "I didn't want to burden you with the added expense of Christmas."

"Hey, Holly, that means Finley's owes you

261

two hundred and fifty dollars," Jake said. "Plus tax. By the way, Mickey, did you tell Mrs. Miracle who you were?" he asked, approaching the two of them. He slipped his arm around Holly's waist and she casually leaned against him.

Mickey shook his head. "Should I have?"

Jake and Holly exchanged a glance, but it was Jake who voiced their question. "How did she know?"

"Know what?" Mickey asked.

"That it was you," Holly said.

"Look, Dad!" Gabe cried out.

Mickey turned his attention to the robot, who walked smartly toward him, stopped and asked in a tinny voice, "When . . . do . . . you . . . go . . . back . . . to . . . Afghanistan?"

Mickey's eyes widened. "How'd you make him say that?"

J.R., who'd been working with Gabe, grinned at Mickey. "I programmed him," Gabe announced proudly. "Mr. Finley helped, but he said I can do it on my own now that I know how."

"You managed to get the robot to do that already?"

"He does all kinds of cool tricks, Dad. Watch."

While Mickey and Gabe were engaged in

programming the robot, Jake and Holly stepped into the kitchen.

"She *couldn't* have known Mickey was Gabe's father." Jake's face was clouded with doubt. "Could she?"

Holly didn't have an answer.

Jake continued, still frowning. "I tried to reach her, but the phone number she listed with HR wasn't in service."

"Then ask her when you see her again," Holly said. Jake had mentioned that, as seasonal help, Emily Miracle would be working until after inventory had been completed in January.

"I won't be able to," Jake told her. "When I went to HR for her personal information, I discovered that she'd handed in her notice. Christmas Eve was her last day."

"But . . ." Holly wanted to argue. Surely Mrs. Miracle would've said *something* at dinner the night before. Things didn't quite add up. . . . And yet, this wonderful woman had done so much to brighten their Christmas.

Before she could comment, the doorbell rang again. Holly chuckled, not even daring to guess who it might be *this* time. Her apartment was turning into Grand Central Station. If she had to guess, the last person to cross her mind would've been . . .

"Lindy!" Her employer's name shot out of Holly's mouth the second she opened the door.

Lindy Lee smiled hesitantly. "I hope I'm not intruding."

"You came, you came." Gabe bounded up from the floor and raced to Lindy Lee's side, taking her hand.

Lindy gave Holly an apologetic look. "Gabe invited me and since I, uh, didn't have any commitments, I thought I'd stop by for a few minutes and wish you all a Merry Christmas." She glanced about the room. "I see you already have a houseful."

"I'm Gabe's father," Mickey said, stepping forward. "Holly's brother." He set his hands on Gabe's shoulders.

"She's the lady I wrote you about," Gabe said, twisting around and looking up at his father. "Isn't she pretty?"

"Yes, she is. . . ." Mickey seemed unable to take his eyes off Lindy Lee.

Holly wouldn't have believed it possible, but Lindy actually blushed.

"Thank you," the designer murmured.

"Make yourself at home," Holly said. "I was just about to serve some eggnog. Would you like a glass?"

"Are you sure it won't be any bother?"

"She's sure," Gabe said, dragging Lindy

Lee toward the couch. "Here, sit next to my dad." He patted an empty space on the sofa. "Dad, you sit here."

Mickey smiled at Lindy Lee. "I guess we've got our orders."

"Yes, sir," Lindy joked, winking at Gabe.

"You know what she said to me, Dad?"

"What?"

"I said," Lindy Lee supplied, "that I need a little boy in my life. A little boy just like Gabe."

Holly wondered if she'd heard correctly. This woman who looked identical to her employer sounded nothing like the Lindy Lee she knew. Gone was the dictatorial, demanding tyrant who ran her fashion-design business with military precision. She'd either been taken over by aliens or Lindy Lee had a gentle side that she kept hidden and revealed only on rare occasions. Like Christmas . . .

An hour later, during a private moment in the kitchen, Jake gave Holly a gift — a cameo that had once belonged to his mother. He said J.R. had given it to him for this very purpose the night before. Holly was thrilled, honored, humbled. She held her breath as he put the cameo on its gold chain around her neck. Holly didn't have anything for him, but Jake said all he wanted was a kiss, and she was happy to comply.

Two hours after that, the small group gathered around the table laden with Christmas fare, including several bottles of exceptional wine brought by Jake and his father. Gabe sat between Mickey and Lindy Lee and chatted nonstop, while J.R. and Jake sat with Holly between them. They took turns saying grace, then took turns again, passing serving dishes to one another.

Amid the clinking of silverware on china and the animated conversation and laughter, Gabe's voice suddenly rose.

"Mrs. Miracle was right," he declared after his first bite of turkey. "This is the *best* Christmas ever."

Emily Merkle reached for her suitcase and started down the long road. Her job in New York was finished, and it had gone even better than she'd expected. Holly and Jake were falling in love. J.R. had more interest in anticipating the future than reliving the pain of the past. Mickey had met Lindy Lee, and Gabe had settled in nicely with his aunt Holly.

Emily hadn't walked far when she was joined by two others, a beautiful woman and a ten-year-old girl. Kaitlyn skipped gracefully at her mother's side, holding

Helene's hand.

"All is well," Emily told the other woman. "J.R. and Jake will celebrate Christmas from now on. It was a big leap for J.R., but once the grandchildren arrive, he will lavish them with love."

"Jake will marry Holly?" she asked.

Emily nodded. "They'll have many years together."

"You chose well for my son."

Emily nodded in agreement. Jake and Holly were a good match and they'd bring out the best in each other.

The other woman smiled contentedly. "Thank you," she whispered.

"It was my pleasure," Emily told her.

And it truly was.

ABOUT THE AUTHOR

Debbie Macomber, the author of *1022 Evergreen Place, 92 Pacific Boulevard, 8 Sandpiper Way,* and *Summer on Blossom Street,* has become a leading voice in women's fiction worldwide. Her work has appeared on every major bestseller list, including those of the *New York Times, USA TODAY,* and *Publishers Weekly.* She is a multiple award winner, and she won the 2005 Quill Award for Best Romance. More than one hundred million of her books have been sold worldwide. For more information on Debbie and her books, visit her Web site, www.DebbieMacomber.com.

We hope you have enjoyed this Large Print book. Other Thorndike, Wheeler, Kennebec, and Chivers Press Large Print books are available at your library or directly from the publishers.

For information about current and upcoming titles, please call or write, without obligation, to:

Publisher
Thorndike Press
295 Kennedy Memorial Drive
Waterville, ME 04901
Tel. (800) 223-1244

or visit our Web site at:

http://gale.cengage.com/thorndike

OR

Chivers Large Print
published by BBC Audiobooks Ltd
St James House, The Square
Lower Bristol Road
Bath BA2 3SB
England
Tel. +44(0) 800 136919
email: bbcaudiobooks@bbc.co.uk
www.bbcaudiobooks.co.uk

All our Large Print titles are designed for easy reading, and all our books are made to last.